"Howard was only alone with you for a moment. One can hardly blame him, you know, for wanting to kiss you. I'd like to myself."

Fearful of frightening her, he pulled her into his arms gently, waiting to see if she objected. When she voluntarily lifted her arms and placed them on his shoulders, he crushed her against him and sought her lips. She felt a pulsating weakness invade her body, yet discovered strength to return the pressure of his lips. For a long moment they clung together, then Monteith lifted his head and gazed at her. An incipient smile lit his eyes.

"That wasn't so bad, was it?"

Fawcett Books
by Joan Smith:

BABE
BATH BELLES
THE BLUE DIAMOND
COUNTRY FLIRT
A COUNTRY WOOING
THE DEVIOUS DUCHESS
LACE FOR MILADY
LADY MADELINE'S FOLLY
LETTERS TO A LADY
LOVE BADE ME WELCOME
LOVER'S VOWS
LOVE'S HARBINGER
RELUCTANT BRIDE
REPRISE
ROYAL REVELS
STRANGE CAPERS
TRUE LADY
VALERIE
WILES OF A STRANGER

COUNTRY FLIRT

Joan Smith

FAWCETT CREST • NEW YORK

A Fawcett Crest Book
Published by Ballantine Books
Copyright © 1987 by Joan Smith

Library of Congress Catalog Card Number: 87-91544

ISBN 0-449-21424-9

Manufactured in the United States of America

First Edition: December 1987

Chapter 1

June was such a lovely month in the countryside of Kent that not even a visit from Lady Monteith could quite destroy the afternoon. Samantha Bright espied the crested carriage crawling up the hill at a pace that told her the check string had already been pulled, and pointed it out to her mother. She took a last approving look at her garden. The sudden hot spell had brought forth a blaze of color. Irises, peonies, and lilies swayed gently before the sentinel row of delphiniums. To her left, the rose bushes stood off to one side—aloof, commanding respectful admiration. Rather like Lady Monteith, Samantha thought.

The horses drew to a stop in front of the Willows, a pretty half-timbered mansion on the crest of the hill. Below, the town of Lambrook spread like a living picture. Houses, horses, carriages, and pedestrians seemed shrunk to an insignificant size, but despite the seeming insignificance, Lambrook was Samantha's world. It was to St. Michael's old Norman church that she went every Sunday to attend the service executed by Reverend Russel. It was along the busy High Street that she visited the shops, met her friends, bought her necessities and a few modest luxuries. The northern limit of her geographical interest was Lambrook Hall, three miles farther along the road, where Lady Monteith lived alone in splendor for most of the year. Lady Monteith's peace was interrupted often by

1

neighbors, occasionally by large house parties, and rarely by one or all of her three sons.

As it was June the fifth, the day after the official closing of the London season, Samantha wondered if Lord Monteith might be with his mama. With this in mind, she tilted her leghorn straw bonnet daringly over her eye, drew off the gardening gloves that were soiled from picking weeds, and wiped the perspiration from her brow. Lord Monteith was not the sort of gentleman to find charm in the homely pursuit of gardening. Indeed, he found only minimal charm in anything rural, as he was a creature of London himself.

"She's getting out," Mrs. Bright said, as the liveried footman hopped down and held the door of the carriage. "Tell Foley to serve tea in the drawing room, Samantha."

Samantha noticed that Lady Monteith came alone, and went with no excitement to order tea. Where would Lord Monteith be the day after the London season finished? Gone on to Brighton, perhaps. Monty often did that. She went to her room to freshen up before taking tea.

As she looked at herself in the mirror, she was just as happy Monty hadn't come to call. Her strawberry-blond hair was all askew, and her face was flushed with the heat. She brushed out her curls and studied the face gazing back at her. At six-and-twenty, she still wore every evidence of youth and some of beauty. Her dark blue eyes were wide set and generously fringed with sooty lashes, lending distinction to a face that was otherwise only pretty. Her short, straight nose was lightly dusted with freckles. With a *tsk* of annoyance for those freckles, she straightened her gown and ran downstairs.

"Ah, Samantha! Come and join us. Lady Monteith was just telling me an intriguing piece of news," Mrs. Bright said. She cocked her head to one side, like a bird, and smiled brightly.

Lady Monteith, with no real social equals in the neighborhood, had chosen Nora Bright as a friend. The widow of a colonel must always be acceptable, and on top of that,

Mrs. Bright's own family was unexceptionable. A little better, in fact, than that of Lady Monteith, née Irene Grimm, daughter of a captain. All this ancient family history had long since been buried under the weight of nobility Irene now carried, of course, but still it was there. The usual condescension of Lady Monteith's manner was noticeably diminished when she called at the Willows.

Samantha had a premonition the intriguing news had to do with Monty, and felt her interest quicken. Engaged! Monty was going to be married! She had always known this news would come one day, and told herself the fluttering in her breast was only natural excitement. Her curtsy was graceful, and her smile undimmed as she made her greeting to her godmother.

"How interesting." She smiled. "What is the news, Lady Monteith?"

Lady Monteith gazed a moment on Nora Bright's daughter. During a life in which little had been denied her, she had failed to gain a daughter. Three rowdy sons, and much good they did her, forever racketing around the countryside, getting into mischief. She carried the hope that Samantha might one day be a daughter-in-law, but it was a hope locked in her own breast. The dowry was insignificant. Her two younger boys must marry money, and as to Monty—well, of course Lord Monteith must look higher than a colonel's daughter. If *he* had no more wits than his papa in that respect, his mother more than made up for it.

"The news? I have just been telling your mother that Lord Howard—my late husband's younger brother—is home from India."

"Is he at Lambrook now?" Samantha asked eagerly.

"No, I had word from Monty that he is in London and will be landing in on me today."

"Is there any special reason for his returning?" Mrs. Bright asked. "I hope he is not ill—one hears such stories of the havoc caused by India's climate."

"It would take more than a monsoon to bother Howard," Lady Monteith said rather irritably. "He has business to settle up with the East India Company today—something to do with his pension, I expect. I hope it is enough to let him set up a place of his own. I don't want him battening himself on me at the Hall."

Mrs. Bright raised an eye bright with mischief and said, "Why, Irene, you used not to be so uncharitable toward Howard. I seem to recall . . ."

"That was long ago, Nora. Once I met Ernest, I realized Howard was a rakehell."

This was French for saying Howard was a younger son. Howard had been her initial quarry, certainly, till she had managed to snare his elder brother and his title.

"Lord Howard was the black sheep of the family, you must know," Lady Monteith added primly. "Oh, he was a handsome fellow, with the sort of raffish appeal of that breed. At least, it appealed to me briefly when I was too young to know better."

Nora Bright gave a knowing look and murmured, "Of course. Now you are *much* older, and wiser."

To prevent the visit from deteriorating into a squabble, Samantha asked, "What did he do in India?"

"He held some junior position with the East India Company, I believe. He seldom wrote home. The only communication we had was parcels of Indian things he used to send from time to time."

"I shouldn't think he'd want to settle in the country," Mrs. Bright said pensively. "Howard was too lively for that."

"Does he have a family with him?" Samantha asked. What she really wanted to follow up was that note from Monteith, but she was patient. It would come in its time. The tea arrived and they settled in to gossip.

"I never heard of his marrying. No, I believe he will be alone. I shall have his Indian junk hauled out of the attics and make him take it with him. Such ugly old debris

4

as he sends across the ocean to litter the Hall. With all the jewels and fine muslin and tea to be had in India, I don't see why he must send us elephants' feet and dangerous-looking weapons. And a stuffed cat! That was really doing it much too brown. I gave it to the last church sale.''

Lady Monteith's fine hazel eyes snapped with anger as she remembered that cat. It had nearly frightened her out of her wits when the carton was unwrapped and there was what looked exactly like a frozen cat staring at her with green glass eyes from a glass case.

''Mrs. Armstrong bought it,'' Samantha mentioned. It had struck her as odd at the time that anyone would pay five shillings for a hideous stuffed tabby.

''Lord Howard should have some lively stories,'' Mrs. Bright mentioned.

''They won't be fit for polite company, but I hope you will come to hear them anyway. Monty says I must do something to welcome Howard. I am having a small dinner party this evening. The sooner the proprieties are taken care of, the sooner I may hint him away.''

''This evening, you say?'' Mrs. Bright asked. ''Oh, dear, I have asked the Russels to dinner.''

''That is all taken care of. I stopped for a word with the vicar in the village. He and his wife will be joining us. That should dampen Howard's enthusiasm if he plans to attach himself to the Hall like a barnacle. I told Mrs. Russel I would tell you.''

Mrs. Bright felt a vestigial trace of rancor at this high-handed way of arranging her life, but on the whole she was curious enough to see Lord Howard again that she didn't object. Much good it would do. Irene ruled the town with an iron fist.

''Who else will be attending?'' she asked.

''Clifford, of course.''

Lady Monteith had been a widow for ten of her fifty-three years. For five of those years, she had given some encouragement to Mr. Clifford Sutton that he might eventually win her hand. As Monty edged past thirty, it was always on her mind that he would marry, and Mr. Sutton's mansion in Lambrook was infinitely preferable to the Dower House. Mr. Sutton was in commerce, but in such a large way that no stain of the merchant colored him. He dealt with bank directors and government boards and members of Parliament, not the general public. Indeed, it was not unknown for him to entertain three cabinet ministers at the same time when he had some new scheme afoot.

"And the Sutton ladies?" Samantha inquired. Clifford had two sisters, no longer Suttons really, but still referred to in the plural by their maiden names for easier conversing.

"Yes, and that about completes the party. Till I see just how bad Howard is, I don't mean to parade him publicly. Oh, and Monty will be with us, I fancy. He had a postscript on the bottom of his note which might have said that. He writes such an abominable hand there is no knowing, but he seems interested in Howard."

Samantha's smile didn't widen by so much as an inch, but her heart beat a little faster and her mind flew to her best gown. She'd sew the new blue ribbon on it for tonight.

With the big news delivered, conversation wandered to the roses, the summer assembly to be held later in June, and the new silks at the drapery shop. After two cups of tea and a slice of Cook's Chinese cake, Lady Monteith rose and left.

"What do you know of this Lord Howard, Mama?" Samantha asked idly, as she filled her cup.

"He was packed off to India before I married. Irene had been walking out with him—quite a catch he was for her, too. Once she caught Lord Monteith's eye, however, she made short shrift of Howard. I don't believe he was ever serious about her. He was running around with some widow lady as well. When Irene nabbed Ernest, the widow

6

connection heated up. India seemed preferable to such an ineligible connection, and his papa sent him away. Howard's major vice was always women. He never could keep his hands off them. But all that would be behind him now— he's much older than I. He must be going on sixty. The Indian climate is very hard on Englishmen. I daresay he's an old relict, come home to die, but he'll not be allowed to do it at Lambrook Hall, poor soul.''

"The Dower House is vacant. She might let him stay there.''

"Much depends on what sort of a gentleman he's become. If he's presentable, Irene might let him have the Dower House. Clifford Sutton will urge her to do it, I daresay. He is such a kind man. I often wonder what he sees in Irene.''

"Perhaps he sees what Irene saw in Ernest—a title.''

"Oh, Clifford is not a climber! He could have a title himself if he wanted one. He allows her to claim him because he is too good-natured to resist.''

"A pity you had not imposed on his good nature first,'' Samantha said, and received a quelling stare. "It should be an interesting evening, in any case. I'm going to sew the new blue ribbons on my gown.''

"I should get busy topping and tailing the gooseberries for Cook, but it makes a shambles of my manicure. I wonder if Monteith will stay in the neighborhood for the assembly,'' Mrs. Bright mentioned idly. She was unaware of any special interest on her daughter's part. Samantha seldom mentioned him.

"I shouldn't think so. It's not for a few weeks. Of course the season is over. . . .''

The season was only a rumor to Samantha. She heard of it, but it might as well take place in India for all it mattered to her. The end of the season usually meant a brief visit home from Monty, of course, and that was of some interest. If he didn't bring guests, he often came to call on her and Mama. He jokingly referred to Sam as his "country flirt." Anyone who had grown up in his shadow realized this was a very poor compliment indeed. Still, even a second-rate compliment from Lord Monteith was secretly cherished.

Mrs. Bright put down her cup and glanced at the casement clock. "Too late to go back to the weeds, and too early to dress for dinner. I believe I'll risk my manicure. We'll be leaving around seven, Samantha."

"I'll be ready." And waiting, she added silently. Really, she had been waiting since Christmas for Monteith's brief visit home. He'd smile and flirt a little, and fly off to London or Brighton or Scotland. Like the rest of her set, she would smile blandly and say, "It was nice to see Monty again." It must be nice to *be* Monty, she thought.

Her life was not arduous, but a single lady with no husband or children was bound to feel dull at times. There seemed no point to her existence. Her few childhood friends had married and moved away, leaving her to find a life amongst her mother's set. She was beginning to settle in too comfortably with the older married folks and widows. Life shouldn't be "comfortable"; it should be exciting, but outside of Monteith's pending visit, the only excitement was the arrival of a dissolute old man home from India. She sighed and went upstairs to sew the bows on her gown.

Chapter 2

Folks in Lambrook were not so fashionable as to arrive late for a dinner party. At seven-thirty that evening, all the guests had assembled in the elegant Rose Saloon at Lambrook Hall. Samantha's first quick survey of the room showed her that Lord Monteith wasn't present. Even before she observed there was no one who could conceivably be Lord Howard, she noticed Monty's absence, and her anticipation of the evening's pleasure diminished. When the ladies were seated, Lady Monteith turned a wrathful eye to the party and exclaimed, "Now, what do you think of this, eh?"

"Lord Howard hasn't come?" Mrs. Bright asked.

"Not come, and he hadn't even the courtesy to write and let me know he has been delayed. I have put this party together for nothing."

The guests blinked to hear their company was valued so low. It was Mr. Sutton who gently hinted to his beloved that she had been brusque. "*We* shall enjoy your dinner, Irene, with or without Lord Howard," he said. It was for his sisters to twitch their shoulders in silent offense.

Lady Monteith smiled in embarrassment and patted Clifford's fingers. Watching, Samantha marveled that Lady Monteith, about the most toplofty person she had ever met, should buckle under to Mr. Sutton, whose origins were lower than her own. He was entirely a self-made man. He was one of those good-natured gentlemen who always found some silver lining in the darkest cloud. Despite his great wealth, he had no pride at all. He was as friendly with the blacksmith as with fine lords and ladies. Everyone agreed his appearance was as amiable as his character—he was of medium height, well built, with dark hair just turning silver around the temples.

"Will Lord Monteith be joining us?" the vicar asked, peering over his spectacles. "I saw him driving through town late this afternoon."

"Monty will be down shortly," his mother said.

Samantha looked down and straightened her gown, for she didn't want anyone to notice that she was smiling. Before long, Lord Monteith appeared at the doorway of the saloon. He surveyed the dull little country party a moment before strolling in to welcome the guests individually, with a smile that was as charming as it was insincere. While he surveyed, Samantha stole a look at him.

It was not Lord Monteith's appearance that had captured her interest. Though tall and elegant, his build was no better than Mr. Sutton's. As he advanced into the room, she noticed that his walk was exceedingly graceful. Everything about him was smooth. There was some poetry in his fluid movements and the seemingly effortless perfection of his toilette. His black evening jacket sat like a second skin on his shoulders, and the intricately arranged cravat was impeccable. Monteith didn't favor the raffish air of the dandy, nor the sporting style of the Corinthian. His simple elegance owed more to the influence of Beau Brummell, and the efforts of a top-notch valet who accompanied him on any overnight trip.

His straw-colored hair was as fine as silk, and as carefully brushed in place as any lady's. Unlike the ladies' hair, his had no curl whatsoever. Samantha watched obliquely as he bowed to the rest of the company before coming to her. Her being last was in no way a slight. As the youngest, and with no title to increase her importance, she was naturally last in precedence. When Lord Monteith bowed and smiled, she decided that she didn't really like him at all. He merely fascinated her because he was different from the local gentlemen.

His smile was polite, no more. There was no hidden love or admiration glowing in his dark blue eyes. His nose was too thin, and his lips wore a permanent expression bordering on disdain. They wore it now as he welcomed her. He seemed to be taking particular note of her freckles, and his speech soon confirmed it.

"You've been out doing battle with the aphids and black rot, I see. You should get yourself a sunbonnet, Sam."

She was mistaken in thinking this denoted disapproval. Monteith was nearly as fond of ladies as his infamous uncle, Lord Howard. He had arranged his circuit of welcome to finish at Samantha's side, that he might flirt with her till dinner was served. That light dusting of freckles put the finishing touch on Sam—what was a country girl without a touch of rusticity? Miss Bright, his sharp eye observed, had other touches of the country as well. Those blue bows, for example, would set a city drawing room to smirking, but they suited Samantha's simple gown admirably.

Samantha ignored his comment. "Well, Monty, I hear you have actually seen Lord Howard. What is he like, and why isn't he here?"

He lifted a well-shaped finger and wagged it playfully. "No, no! First you must tell me how happy you are to see me again. My pride demands it."

"Naturally we are all *aux anges* at the condescension of your sojourn."

"Say, rather, 'visit.' 'Sojourn' implies an indefinite stay. I shall definitely be removing *aussitôt que possible*. As soon as Uncle Howard deigns to appear, that is to say.

11

One must not be behindhand in welcoming the family ancients."

"One might even go so far as to stay a few days."

"That is overdoing it, surely. I want to make him feel welcome, not honored. And by the by, you haven't asked me to take a seat."

"Take all you want. They're yours."

"Why do I feel you're doing me a favor, I wonder?" he asked, and drew a petit-point chair close to hers.

"Your London flirts are more effusive, I assume?"

"Effusive suggests to me an overflowing, almost a gushing. Your welcome is mean-spirited at best. And now that I have been made to feel *de trop* in my own saloon, you may inquire for the guest of honor."

"Thank you. I am dying to—"

Monteith lifted his hand, palm down, to stop her. "My manners have already begun to fall off. Before we proceed to Lord Howard, I must compliment you on your appearance." He regarded her closely, his eyes falling from her face to study her toilette. "Not the gown—that would be doing it too brown," he said with a mischievous twinkle; then his eyes returned to her face. "Ah, I have it! You're ageless, Sam. You always look the same."

"You make me sound like a mountain, or an octogenarian! If that is your notion of a compliment, I thank you for the intention."

"It was meant as one, I promise you."

"At my advanced years to 'always look the same' must be a great consolation. After going to the bother of wearing a strawberry mask for two mornings and running and visiting the coiffeur last week, however, I rather expected some such inanity as looking 'better than usual.'"

"We shall blame it on the provincial coiffeur. I stick by my original assessment—always the same, in both appearance and tartness of tongue."

Her lips quivered in amusement. "You're still the same, too, Monteith."

He regarded her warily. "Thank you, I think. That will teach me to tell a lady the truth. I should have been prattling of 'charming new hairdo' and gown 'in the highest kick of fashion,' I daresay."

"No, no, such barefaced lies are unnecessary. Only a little ingenuity in coating the pill of truth is all I ask. We expect no less of the parish's most eligible bachelor."

"What will you do for a compliment when I'm shackled, Sam?"

She hunched her shoulders in indifference. "Fade away to a shadow, cock up my toes, and die."

"You should have gone to London when you were still—that is—"

She looked at him wide-eyed. "I was going to, but it was considered unsafe. The roads were menaced by Vikings and Goths in those days."

Monteith touched her chin with one long finger. "Don't go overboard on the sarcasm, Sammie. You're not old enough to be playing Madame de Staël. Only established matrons who wear blue stockings are permitted to be clever. You must find yourself a husband first. It is a sine qua non in polite society. Ladies still on the catch for a man must simper and smile. It would help if you could learn to blush."

"Difficult! You can't teach an old dog new tricks." She laughed.

"And you must not reveal that you find us gentlemen absurd."

"Impossible!"

"Then you're doomed to the shelf for life."

"Fine. Are we all finished with the *compliments* now? I am dying to hear what Lord Howard is like and why he isn't here."

He shook his head. "Much must be missing in your life, when you encroach on the death metaphor for such a paltry excuse. Young maidens are allowed to be 'dying' only in the cause of romance. He's as tanned as a blackamoor, and has wretched manners. I believe that answers your two questions. But never mind Howard. *I* am here to entertain you.''

On this speech, he drew his chair a little closer and lowered his voice. ''Tell me all the *on-dits*,'' he ordered, and seemed truly interested to hear them.

Samantha didn't want to make the summer assembly the first item of priority, and said, ''Reverend Russel is having the summer fête next week. A fête champêtre we are calling it this year, as he's upped the price to a crown. We're holding it here at the Hall.''

He nodded approvingly. ''We wouldn't want to cheapen the Hall by letting them in for pennies. It all sounds very French. Champagne and strawberries, I expect? Flower-strewn swings and ladies with broad-brimmed hats. Young couples dallying along the riverbanks. Charming. Some-one should paint it. A pity Fragonard is no longer alive.''

''Strawberries and clotted cream, actually, and of course the smock race and egg race and three-legged race. You don't have a river on the estate, but the children will likely be wading for frog spawn in the stream.''

Monteith lowered his brow and frowned in mock anger. ''You *haven't* changed a bit, Miss Bright. Still playing the country lumpkin to the top of your bent, to make me appear a fop. Tell me, am I having a ball afterward?''

''No, a barn dance, milord.''

The flash of amusement in his dark eyes reminded Sa-mantha what it was she liked about Monty. He was always willing to laugh at himself and anyone else who deserved it. But it wasn't a mean laugh. He merely enjoyed the oddities of the world.

''What other earthly delights await me in the country? No need to take me literally and inform me of worms and toads and dandelions.''

''The summer assembly is at the end of the month, if you're still here. I doubt that would appeal to one of your jaded appetites. No doubt Brighton would provide a better party than Lambrook. On the other hand," she added with exaggerated importance, "they've put a new coat of paint on the raised platform in the assembly room at the inn. Can Brighton boast of a green raised platform?"

"Not even Prinney's Pavilion has such magnificence! And the music?"

"Jed Flood and his Fiddlers Three, with Mrs. Flood at the pianoforte, as usual."

"Tempting! But enough of these paltry details. What of the ladies? Has Lambrook any new pulchritude to tempt a jaded palate? If there's one thing dearer to my heart than money, it is the ladies. Not just any old woman, mind you, but a prime piece of pulchritude."

Samantha shook her head in sad resignation. So far as she could tell, Monty cared not a fig for money or virtue or character or any of the items the generality of mankind admired. She couldn't count the number of items she had heard him say, "Yes, but is she pretty?" when a deb had been nudged forward for his consideration. "How are her eyes, her teeth, her ankles?"

Excellence in any of the above was always sufficient recommendation. The lady need not be incomparable. Indeed, from what she had seen of some of his "beauties" at the Hall, he could discover charms invisible to a less keen eye. A certain Mrs. Higgs, for example, was a butter-toothed widow with a dumpy frame, but Monty saw only her long lashes and dimples. The eyes were well enough, but as for the dimples, they weren't on her face or arms.

She scoured her mind and said, "Well, there's Mrs. Armstrong, a new widow lady who has rented the old brick house across from us on High Street."

"Is she pretty?" he asked, with every appearance of interest.

"She'll be at your barn dance, Monty. Why don't you go and see for yourself?"

"Will you save me a waltz?"

"I feel safe in promising you every waltz. That city dissipation hasn't reached Lambrook yet."

"That explains your unusual generosity! Perhaps I'll have a waltzing party and teach it to the locals. This Mrs. Armstrong—where is she from?"

"What does it matter? She has lovely black hair and long lashes."

Monteith tilted his head and massaged his chin. It was at Samantha's long lashes that he gazed, smiling softly. What a pretty girl she was! And what would her dowry be? She might make an excellent wife for one of his brothers. She would be a lively addition to the family gatherings. He might even bring her into fashion in London.

The butler announced dinner, and Monteith went to do his duty in escorting ladies to the dining room. They were one gentleman short. The vicar had his wife, Mr. Sutton's sisters each had a husband with them, and Lady Monteith had Mr. Sutton, which permitted Monteith to escort both the Brights.

Lady Monteith looked with annoyance at her lovely table. She'd have to do the pretty all over again when Howard took it into his head to come. No matter, with Monty home, the house would be full of company. She was of a quiet disposition, without being an actual hermit. There wasn't much she enjoyed more than a quiet evening alone, or with Clifford, who wasn't a roisterous sort of man.

Dinner proceeded quietly for two courses. The roast of lamb was just being placed on the board when there was a raucous hollering heard in the front hall. "Holloa, boy! Boy!" The sound reverberated through the house, followed by a rattle as of a box falling.

"Good gracious! What is that?" Lady Monteith demanded.

Her son smiled at the assembled party. "It sounds as

16

though Uncle Howard has come to dinner after all. No need to disturb yourself, Mama,'' he said to his motionless parent. ''I'll do the pretty and welcome him.''

He rose languorously and glided from the room.

Chapter 3

A moment later Lord Monteith reappeared with his uncle, Lord Howard. Every eye in the room gleamed with avid curiosity as it turned to see the infamous black sheep. Samantha looked, and felt a nearly overwhelming urge to laugh at the striking similarity between nephew and uncle. Lord Howard looked as if someone had taken Monty into a tanning factory and treated him. The general face and figures were similar, but the uncle's skin was darker and coarser. He was obviously older, more dissipated, more wrinkled, and heavier than Monteith. His hairline had receded an inch or so, but the eyes that surveyed the room had the same youthful gleam. The head sat at the same proud angle. Lord Howard's toilette lacked the elegance of the younger man's; Stultz had padded his shoulder wider than necessary and nipped the waist in too tightly.

When Lord Howard spoke, the strange feeling of similarity faded. His accents were not the cultured ones of his nephew, nor were his words as polite, though they showed some concern for the company. "Good evening, all. I'm Lord Howard, the nabob. Don't interrupt your eating on my account. I'll just slide into any empty chair and will soon catch up with you."

As he spoke, he glanced around the table and spotted the vacant chair. Before taking up his seat, he turned to one of the hovering footmen. "I'm ravenous as a lion. I haven't had a bite since noon. Bring me a platter of meat, lad. Hop, hop.''

Then he sat down and began a perusal of the female faces that surrounded the table. The sharp-eyed dame at the head of the table—that would be Irene, of course. She used to be a good-looking lass when she married Ernie. The ladies lasted a little better here than in the tropics. She didn't look over fifty, which she must be. She'd married Ernest thirty-six years ago.

"Lord Howard, I'm happy you could make it for dinner," Lady Monteith said, through thin lips.

"Ho, I'd forgotten you keep country hours. We dine after nine in India. The heat, you know. We live half our lives in the dark. It's that or be parboiled. I'd have been here hours ago if that demmed *dubash* I left off at John Company's office in London hadn't detained me by getting himself lost. I brought him along to England to handle my affairs with the company, to save me from pelting off to the city. Well, Irene, you're holding up well for a lady of your years." He smiled.

Lady Monteith ignored this two-edged compliment. "Pray allow me to introduce you to my guests," she said stiffly, and ran around the table, mentioning everyone's name. While she performed this thankless job, Lord Howard reached out and grabbed a piece of bread, which he buttered and ate in great bites. He glanced up from time to time to acknowledge introductions with a brief nod.

Then a plate of mutton was placed before him. He squared his elbows, lowered his head, and tore into it. The sight reminded Lady Monteith of nothing so much as a wild animal at a carcass. She winced and shook her head at her son, that paragon of suavity, who smiled blandly.

Other than making a spectacle of himself, Lord Howard proved a bore while at his meal. He conversed little. Any question was answered curtly, often with no more than a nod or shake of his head. When he had cleaned two plates, he sat back, patted his stomach, and said to Lady Monteith, "That's more like it! Your *sircar* sets a very decent table, Sis."

"Thank you," she said, in icy accents.

The man was impossible. She would not submit her guests to the sight of him gobbling his food again. He must be hinted away at once. "That fellow you left in London handling your business, Lord Howard—"

"Call me Howard, Sis. Now that I am home in the bosom of my family, we may leave off with titles. I may be a burra sahib, but plain Howard is good enough for me. That would be Rangi you're talking about. My *dubash*."

The words "bosom of my family" smote her with grim forebodings. "He's arranging your pension with the East India Company, is he?" she asked.

"Oh, I have no pension. I left John Company eons ago."

"No pension! But—"

"Nay, I've been working for the nawabs. Rangi will be spending some time at the *hoppo*, getting my goods through customs, but we should see him within the week."

She ignored the annoying and unnecessary use of foreign words and tried to ignore that "within the week." "Would it not have gone more quickly if you had done it yourself?" she asked tartly.

"A burra sahib must learn to delegate authority, or he'd spend his days looking over piddling invoices and bills. Rangi is a sharp lad. I trained him up myself."

"But still," she persisted, "I think you ought to go back to London, at once."

Lord Monteith looked from mother to uncle and smiled a languid smile. "Why, Mama, you will be giving Howard the notion he isn't welcome in the bosom of his family."

She glared down the table at her son and said nothing. Monteith accepted a piece of fruit from the footman and turned his attention once again to his uncle. "We would be most interested to hear something of your sojourn in India, Uncle," he said.

Looking at Monty, Samantha saw the glitter of mischief in his dark eyes. What an obstinate man he was, encouraging this farouche relative, when it was as clear as water his mother disapproved.

Lord Howard said, "It was hot and crowded and dirty." Then he accepted a piece of melon and attacked it with his knife. "You couldn't get a decent melon in India. They were all watery and tasteless—like this one, Sis," he added, and pushed it away. He beckoned to the footman and took up an orange to try his luck with it.

"Mind you," he ran on, "they have a fruit there called mangosteen that beats anything here in England all hollow. The most exquisite thing I ever tasted. The table fare was tolerable, once I taught my lads not to douse everything in oil. The fish and poultry were excellent."

"How did you find the ladies, Uncle?" Monteith asked leadingly.

Lord Howard frowned, for he took this subject even more seriously than his food, and that is saying a good deal. "A trifle dusky, of course," he said. His glance slid to Samantha and rested a moment on her blond curls. "They were well enough. The color of a hen is irrelevant, so long as she produces eggs. *My* woman—"

Lady Monteith paled visibly, and when she spoke, her voice was hollow. "You didn't *marry* one of them! You didn't bring her home!"

"I didn't marry Jemdanee," he said sadly. "I gave some thought to it. She was as gentle and affectionate a girl as ever lived. I might have married her, but then when our son died, she went off on her looks."

The vicar's fork fell to the table with a clatter, which helped to cover the sound of strangled gasps from the Sutton ladies.

Lord Howard threw up his shoulders and sighed. "I set Jemdanee and her family up in a house before I left. Not

21

a *cutcha* either, but a proper *chunam*, built with mortar in place of mud. I had a rattan veranda thrown up to block the sun and all. I had an eye for her little sister, but her papa was asking five hundred sicca rupees for her. That would be over fifty pounds."

The vicar cleared his throat, and his wife fanned herself vigorously. Lord Howard noticed and said, "You need not fear I've returned a Hindu. I'm still a Christian, Reverend. You'll see me decorating the family pew come Sunday."

At every mention of future dates, Lady Monteith squirmed visibly.

"A man who has a taste for feminine companionship would do well to consider marriage," Reverend Russel felt obliged to say.

"Women are much on my mind," Lord Howard assured him. "I will be looking sharp about me for a replacement for Jemdanee."

"Howard!" Lady Monteith objected. All the other guests looked extremely uncomfortable.

"Now what has set you to gasping like a bunch of stuck pigs?" Lord Howard demanded. "We are talking about *marriage*, ain't we?" As he spoke, he turned his gaze to examine the specimens of English womanhood around the table.

The Sutton ladies stared at him as if he were a yahoo, and were very thankful they had the protection of their husbands. Mrs. Bright was the next to fall under his gaze. Samantha's mother was a pretty, delicate lady, bright of eye, dainty in her movements. She was plenty young enough for Lord Howard. Indeed, she considered his fifty-plus years too old to be of interest to her. "Your name was Nora something, if I ain't mistaken?" he asked.

"Yes, Nora Bright."

"I made sure I recognized those eyes, but I can't quite recall—are you married?" he asked.

"I am a widow," she answered with tolerable composure.

22

"Ah, well, that lets you out," he said bluntly. "And this pretty little lassie is your girl, is she?" he asked, turning to examine Samantha.

"My daughter, Samantha." She nodded.

"A blonde is a welcome change to me after India," he said, and studied Samantha as if she were a painting. "A nice full cheek, teeth in good repair—a fine buxom lass. Nay, don't blush, missie." He laughed. "I shan't say a word about your figure, though between you and me and the milk jug, I haven't seen one finer since I left the theater last night."

Bewildered, she said, "Thank you," and looked helplessly around the table.

"High praise, Uncle," Monty said. "Can I offer you some wine to kill the taste of that sour orange?"

Lord Howard shook his head. "It would take more than wine. I've brought some mangosteen seeds back with me. We'll plant them in our conservatory tomorrow."

Lady Monteith girded her loins for battle. "The conservatory is full."

"You may root out these tasteless melons, if that is where they came from." Howard reached for a handful of nuts and began cracking them with his bare hands. Between cracking and popping them into his mouth, he turned his attention to the Sutton ladies. "You two girls have managed to trap a husband before now, I daresay?" he asked.

They were extremely relieved to be able to point to their respective spouses. "There is no accounting for taste," Lord Howard mumbled, and made four new enemies.

Reverend Russel felt severe qualms about having this rake loose in his village. "We have several nice widows in Lambrook," he said.

Lord Howard shook his head sadly. "Christian though I am, I must say I admire the Hindu's custom of suttee. Once a woman's husband is dead, what is left for her? She's fulfilled the role she was put on the earth for. She

23

is nothing but a weight on the rest of society having to support her. No woman should have to suffer such degradation as that.''

"Lord Howard!" Mr. Sutton gasped, and looked to the love of his life, the widowed Lady Monteith. "I never heard anything so barbaric in my life! It was my understanding the English are eliminating that savage custom of incinerating widows on the funeral pyre!"

"Trying to, but the ladies keep leaping into the flames despite our efforts. It is wrong for us to try to impose our customs on them. They have their own religion. There's nothing left for those widows, when all is said and done. Who would want another man's leavings?"

"Surely the widows don't go *willingly*?" Samantha asked.

"They're raring to be grilled—some of them."

"What about the others?" she asked, staring in disbelief.

"They take a little persuading."

"But what happens to their children?" Mrs. Bright asked.

"The family takes care of them. It is a family's duty to care for all its members, in India as here in England."

Lady Monteith found this idea even more distasteful than suttee. "As you just pointed out, Lord Howard, one must not try to impose foreign customs on another land. Here in England, it is *chacun pour soi*. A fully grown man would hardly expect to batten himself on his family."

"I'm sure Lord Howard is referring to helpless family members, largely women and children," the reverend mentioned. "You will find most civilized religions promote respect for the family."

Lord Howard nodded. "Suttee is the widow's means of showing respect for her late husband," he explained. "And, of course, purdah is also practiced out of respect, but—"

The reverend looked interested. "That is the custom of

24

secluding the women from public observation, I believe? It seems a bit extreme to me, but there is no harm in it, I daresay, if it is a Hindu tradition.''

"They go too far with this purdah business." Lord Howard scowled.

Samantha stared, and when she decided he was serious, she felt a laugh rise up in her throat. "I see," she said, "killing ladies is fine, but hiding them from sight goes too far."

"How are we expected to get a look at them, enshrouded with curtains as they are?" Lord Howard asked. "Mind you, there is something to be said for a pair of flashing dark eyes glimpsed over a veil. But they ain't one, two, three with those sapphires in your face, missie."

"My daughter is only twenty-six, Lord Howard," Mrs. Bright felt obliged to tell him.

He examined her with interest. "I can see she ain't over the hill. You don't look over twenty, either, my dear. Still in the first flush of youth. I'm amazed Monteith here hasn't nabbed you before now."

Monteith looked down the table and examined Samantha closely, with a smile lighting his dark eyes. "I have been rather remiss in that respect," he said.

"That you have," Lord Howard warned him. "A lad your age should have had his nursery started long ago. I'm sure the vicar here will agree with me that a man's purpose for being on the earth is to get married and raise a family."

"None of us would dare to disagree," Monteith said, "and I expect that by the time I am *your* age, Uncle, I will have done what I was put here to do."

"Aye, you may sneer at me if you will, laddie, but there is a difference in our situations. You are the eldest son, born into your wealth and position. I had my fortune to make. A man don't get a million pounds in the bank by hampering himself with a wife and family. And in India, you know, the choice of ladies was severely limited."

Lord Howard continued for some time in this vein. Most of his auditors heard not a word after the magical phrase "a million pounds."

When he finally fell silent, Lady Monteith beckoned the footman. "Fetch some champagne, Rutley," she said. "We must have champagne to welcome his lordship home from abroad, into the bosom of his family." Then she smiled benignly down the board. "Howard, my dear, tell me more about that magazine fruit seed you brought for our conservatory. We shall root out the oranges tomorrow and plant it. Such fun!"

Lord Monteith leaned toward Samantha and said in a low voice, unsteady with laughter, "You shan't have to purchase *La Belle Assemblée* next year, Sam. Mama will give you a copy from her magazine tree."

He looked, expecting her to riposte. Her eyes were riveted on Lord Howard. A peculiar little smile lifted her lips. The future suddenly looked wildly interesting, with this untamed and exotic animal running loose in town. After a moment, she turned to him. "Pardon me, did you say something, Monteith?"

"Nothing of any account," he replied. His disgruntled expression told her he was peeved, but she was too interested in watching Lady Monteith's shameless about-face to bother with Monteith at that moment.

Chapter 4

It never for a moment occurred to Lord Howard that his family didn't know to what famous heights he had risen. In India everyone knew Burra Sahib Lord Howard. Rather than vex him, Lady Monteith's brusque manner told him she was the same proud woman she had always been. He respected her for it, and when her manner warmed so noticeably at the tail end of dinner, he assumed she had been bowled over by his stimulating presence. After a few glasses of champagne and a million playful questions about India, the ladies retired to the saloon to leave the gentlemen to their port.

It was, unfortunately, impossible for Lady Monteith to give full rein to her joy with Clifford Sutton's sisters in the room. She confined herself to lesser exclamations of delight and amazement.

"Can you believe it?" she asked. "A million pounds, and he as close to an ape as makes no difference."

Mrs. Tucker, the younger Sutton lady, said, "There is a prime parti for some lucky young lady! He likes them young, Irene. Why, I do believe he was casting lures in Miss Bright's direction."

Mrs. Jenkins, the elder Sutton lady, was made of more clever stuff. "We must take him to call on Cousin Alvinia Morrison," she mentioned.

Lady Monteith quickly assessed the situation and came

to her own conclusions. Lord Howard was not a day less than fifty-five. He was only a year younger than her own late husband. A man of that age, especially one who had been subjected to years of the pestilence and fevers of India, was no fit husband for anyone. He must remain single, and he must remain at Lambrook Hall, where she could keep an eye on his million pounds. What a boon for the younger boys, Teddie and Bert. Monty must discover where they were visiting and order them home at once.

"Whomever he marries," Mrs. Bright said, "I hope she doesn't survive him, for I don't doubt he'll put in his will she must perish on his funeral pyre."

"Such a whimsical sense of humor as he has." Lady Monteith smiled. Already it had darted into her head that but for Howard's dread of widows, she might make a pitch for him herself.

Mrs. Russel listened and added her mite. "We should get our heads together and find him a wife, ladies, or we will have havoc in the parish. There is no denying he is a little—" She intercepted a scathing glance from her hostess and began to mumble. "So long in India. Only natural, I'm sure, but he *did* say 'my son,' Irene, and he was not married."

"The son is dead—thank goodness. Excuse me, ladies. I must see to his apartment."

Lady Monteith went after the housekeeper. "The small yellow room tucked under the eaves is no longer sufficient for Lord Howard, Mrs. Gaines. Put him in the best guest suite."

"Lord Monteith already told me, before his lordship's arrival."

"Before his arrival! Then he knew all along and let me make a cake of myself. Wretched boy!"

"Where am I to put all his slaves?" Mrs. Gaines asked. "He brought a dozen servants home with him. All wearing bed sheets. They must do their own laundry, milady. I have only the one dolly."

"Put them in the attic. Oh, dear! You must bring the elephant's foot and the swords down to the saloon. Get them now, Mrs. Gaines, before he joins us."

There was a very undignified scrambling around of servants depositing Indian lumber about the Rose Saloon, where it looked as out of place as a dog in church amidst the elegant traditional furnishings. There was no time to hang the assorted swords. Four of them stood against the marble fireplace, crossed on either side of the grate. An Indian blanket was tossed over the best cut-velvet sofa; knives and brass pots were scattered at random.

Samantha watched in amusement. "A pity you gave the stuffed cat away," she mentioned. "Lord Howard might miss it."

"Bother! You're right. He'll certainly be asking for it. I wonder who bought it."

"Mrs. Armstrong," Samantha told her.

Before more could be said, the gentlemen came trooping into the saloon to join the ladies. Lord Howard's rough voice was easily distinguishable above the more polite accents. "So they rode all night and were at Lob Lob Creek before morning," he said in his carrying voice. "They got into sampans, and the prostitutes came right on board, for the Chinese are very strict about that sort of thing, you know, unlike India. It was the only place . . ."

A pretty maid hustled past the group as they crossed the hall, and Lord Howard's attention was distracted. "There goes a saucy little stern if I ever saw one." He smiled and nudged Monteith in the ribs.

Reverend Russel wiped his brow and wondered how soon he could leave. He had never before had the job of upbraiding a millionaire for his libertine ways. It was not a chore he looked forward to with any pleasure.

Lord Howard stopped at the doorway and looked all round the Rose Saloon. "It is just as I remember it," he said. Then he stepped in and picked from the table a knife that Lady Monteith hadn't found time to display more artfully. "Ah, Irene! I am happy you kept my *creese* safe for me. This knife nearly killed me. I kept it to remind me of my mortality. A band of banditti attacked me one night in a dark alley. I wrestled this *creese* from one of them and stuck it between the bleater's ribs."

"Really, Lord Howard!" Mrs. Russel said weekly, and looked to her husband.

"Self-defense," he explained. "It was my money or him." He strolled to the fireplace and picked up a scimitar to flail the air a moment.

At fifty-five years, the nabob was still a handsome man. All the ladies except Mrs. Russel were struck by what a dashing figure he cut, with his weathered face and reckless manner, as he narrowly missed shattering priceless objets d'art.

Samantha heard a low voice in her ear. "Quite a corsair!" Looking up, she saw Monteith had strolled along beside her. For perhaps the first time in her life, she hadn't been aware of his presence when they were in the same room.

He took up a seat beside her, and while Lord Howard performed for the ladies with the scimitar and *creese,* showing them how one was held in the teeth, the other in the hand, they talked.

"Did you know what he was like, Monty? Your mother said you'd met Lord Howard in London."

"I was very much surprised with his manners this evening," he assured her. "In London, he behaved rather badly, I fear."

"As opposed to his genteel performance here?"

"Precisely. I shan't be able to show my face at the Green Room at Covent Garden for another decade. A certain Mrs. Grimes took umbrage at his proposal—or do I mean proposition?"

"Probably the latter. You *did* say *Mrs.* Grimes."

"There was a ring involved, at any rate. A great lump of diamond the size of an acorn. I wonder if Uncle brought his jewelry collection to the Hall with him. He showed it to me in London.''

Lord Howard was performing a particularly lively lunge at an invisible enemy. Samantha watched, smiling, and didn't reply. When the invisible enemy lay dead on the floor, she turned to Monteith. ''What were you saying?''

''I fear I have done Lambrook a bad turn, bringing Uncle here.''

''Whatever about the others, *I* thank you, Monteith. He will be a very lively addition to our circle. Unlike yourself, he plans to make a sojourn of it. When will you be off?''

''I daren't trust the Public Enemy amongst my family and friends without me here to control him. I shall make a sojourn after all.''

To save her saloon from complete annihilation, Lady Monteith suggested another round of champagne.

''Not for me, thankee,'' Lord Howard said, and set the sword back against the grate. ''Rich food always makes me bilious. I shall have a glass of cold water and go up to bed.''

''Are you not feeling well, dear Howard?'' Lady Monteith asked. The edge of hope that tinged her solicitude was hardly noticeable.

''It is my old complaint acting up on me. Dyspepsia. If ice water don't cure it, a glass of soda water will. If you will just ask that saucy little serving wench of yours—the one with the red curls—to bring the water to my chamber, I will make my bows now.'' He bobbed his head and left.

''I'll attend to it, Mama,'' Monteith said, and went to inform his butler the maids were not to go near Lord Howard's room, but if one of the footmen would be so kind as to take him up a glass of soda water, he would appreciate it.

As soon as the guest of honor was safely beyond earshot, Lady Monteith began hinting Clifford and his sisters away, to allow her a good coze with the Brights, who were her particular bosom bows. One must have someone to discuss the matter with, and she knew Monty was not the one. After half an hour, she had accomplished her aim and could settle in for some blunt scheming.

She ordered a fresh tea tray, and the ladies sat with their heads together, while Monty lounged idly in his chair, listening.

"I wonder if this dyspepsia thing is likely to be serious," was Lady Monteith's first remark.

Her son smiled his enigmatic smile and clucked. "One would almost think you hoped so, Mama," he chided.

"This is no time to be satirical, Monty. The man is worth a cool million. He'll snap up the first lady who will have him, and Teddie and Bert may kiss the fortune goodbye. It is our duty to try to secure it for them. Howard has strong family feelings. I'm sure his fortune will be left to the family if we can prevent his marrying an outsider."

"A pity he dislikes widows, or you might toss your bonnet at him yourself, Mama," her disobliging son sneered.

"I swear he had an eye for you, Nora, till he found out you had been married," Lady Monteith said to Mrs. Bright.

"You may be sure I have no interest in a gentleman of his kidney!" Nora exclaimed in shock.

"Nor he in a lady past twenty," Monteith added. "You must have noticed it was Sam he was ogling." This was taken as a joke. It was too farfetched to take seriously. Everyone but Samantha laughed aloud. She smiled, but there was an edge of smugness in her look.

"If Lord Howard's age did not make him ineligible for me, you may be sure his character does!" Samantha exclaimed. "He had a son in India."

"But he is dead," Lady Monteith added happily.

"That was long ago and in another land," Monteith added satirically. No one paid him any heed.

His mother continued. "Imagine the old fool building a

house for that Jem woman. I wonder who else he has squandered his money on.''

"I believe it is his jewelry he scatters upon the females, not money," Monty told her. "He has a fabulous collection of jewels, Mama. He took a handful of rings to the Green Room at Covent Garden last night."

The lady turned quite pale. "You never mean it! What on earth did you take him to the Green Room for? You know what sort of creatures he would run into there."

"I expect that is precisely why he filled his pockets with gems. I didn't exactly take him, however. There was no keeping him away. I merely accompanied him in the role of watchdog, and limited his gifts to one."

"We must under no account let him return to London," Lady Monteith said firmly. "Here in Lambrook there is no one to give his rings to. Or, at least, we would hear of it and bring it to a stop pretty quickly."

For no reason she could put a finger on, Samantha's thoughts turned to Mrs. Armstrong.

"He's hell-bent on marrying," Monteith said thoughtfully. "It was all he talked of yesterday afternoon."

"A man doesn't go to a Green Room at the theater to find a wife," his mother pointed out.

"A last bit of a frolic before he was caught in parson's mousetrap was the way he described it," Monty told her. "I felt his frolics were best played out in the city. He's serious about marriage, Mama, and what we should do is import some of our spinster cousins to have a go at him."

Lady Monteith considered this a moment. "If I could be sure Edith is past her breeding years, I'd invite her," she said. "She always claimed Teddie is her heir. The Russels will be at him to get married and settle down."

"I don't believe Edith will turn the trick," Monteith said. "A dry moralist of more than forty years will not tempt Howard—or anyone else. The lady must be lively, pretty, and youngish. I'll cudgel my brains and think of someone."

"You might think of someone for yourself while you're about it," his mother said grimly. "He called *you* to task for still being single. We don't want to do anything to give him a disgust of us."

"In which case you must turn Mr. Sutton off, Mama," her son retaliated.

"You don't think he was serious about suttee?" Samantha asked.

Monty regarded her quizzically. "He doesn't plan to try to introduce the custom to England, but he does appear to have a distinct aversion to widow ladies—as wives, I mean. In a mistress, widowhood is no objection. We must confine our bridal candidates to spinsters."

"Perhaps if he took a mistress . . ." Lady Monteith said thoughtfully.

Again Samantha thought of Mrs. Armstrong. She nearly uttered the name, till she remembered no actual evidence suggested the woman might be of the muslin company. She didn't openly consort with gentlemen, at least, though there was a certain something in the flash of her eye and the sway of her hips that suggested it. The feeling was widespread in Lambrook. Mrs. Russel was the only lady who had called on her for purely social reasons. A few others had dropped in to have their tea leaves read. Mrs. Russel did some amateur reading of the leaves. She did not accept money for it, but was known to welcome flowers or food.

"But then, there is all the lovely jewelry," Lady Monteith added after a little pause. "We may kiss that goodbye if he takes up with a lightskirt. And he'd build her a house, too, very likely. So vexing, one hardly knows what to do."

Monty cleared his throat and uttered a speech that had the awful ring of truth to it. "I rather think you distress yourself for nothing, Mama. The burra sahib will do as he demmed well pleases."

After a good deal more discussion, the Brights went

home, and Lady Monteith went to bed to continue scheming. She mentally drew up a schedule of items to be accomplished. She must discover just how strong Howard's constitution was. Her hope was that his stomach was gone entirely and he would survive only a year or so. India was a well-known destroyer of constitutions, and, really, the meal that bothered him that night was not extraordinarily rich.

If he seemed strong, she must find him a lady too old to breed, but still young enough to be attractive. Preferably this unique lady would be a cousin guaranteed to leave her portion to either Teddie or Bert upon her own demise. And in the meanwhile, she must find him a local mistress, to keep him away from the pernicious Green Room. She would also make life at Lambrook Hall so delightful that he would be in no hurry either to marry or go to London. And she'd set Monty on to finding Teddie and Bert, too, only she knew they were touring the Lake District with friends, and finding them might take weeks.

Only after all this had been settled did she finally close her eyes and sleep.

Chapter 5

At nine-thirty the next morning the door knocker sounded in the Bright household. Social calls at such an hour were unknown, so the Brights were astonished to hear Lady Monteith's voice in the hallway. Within thirty seconds, Lady Monteith and her son were shown into the breakfast parlor, where the ladies were discussing last night's party over a second cup of coffee.

"Irene! What brings you out at such an hour!" Mrs. Bright exclaimed. "I hope there is nothing amiss at the Hall?"

"Everything is amiss at the Hall," was the comprehensive reply.

"Sit down and have some coffee."

Monteith took a chair beside Samantha while her mother poured and she outlined the problem.

"It is that cursed stuffed cat!" was the first exasperated speech. "Howard has been asking for it, even before he left his room this morning. It seems it saved his life in Calcutta. Some banditti entered his room one night to stab him, and one of them stepped on the cat's tail. The cat awoke and yelped, thus alerting Howard. What idiotic idea must he take into his head but to have the thing stuffed when it died, and send it home to the Hall."

Monteith's eyes glinted with amusement, and he said aside to Samantha, "The cat's name is Ginger. We do not call it the 'cursed stuffed cat' in front of Howard, you understand. I mention it in case the subject should arise—as I fear it will. Mama tells me you think Mrs. Armstrong has Ginger. The lady, if memory serves, also has 'lovely black hair and long lashes.' "

"Yes, she's the woman I mentioned to you last night. She's new in the parish—she came in April."

His eyebrow rose a trifle in question. "Woman or lady?"

Samantha hesitated. "I don't know that she isn't a lady," she admitted. "She lives in a decent house and has servants."

"So do the more successful members of the muslin company. The purpose of our visit to town this morning is to retrieve Ginger. Do you call on Mrs. Armstrong? Mama doesn't seem to have her acquaintance, which makes our visit awkward. We had hoped you might introduce us."

"No, we don't know her."

"Then I assume she is not accepted as a lady."

Samantha frowned over this social puzzle. "She doesn't go to church, you see, or we would have met her. She keeps rather to herself. Mrs. Russel called once, and Mrs. Armstrong never repaid the visit, which was taken as a wish for privacy. A few other ladies left their cards, and none was returned." Samantha hunched her shoulders.

"And so Mrs. Armstrong has been gossiped into the social wilderness," Monty said. "I have noticed the more attractive women often suffer that fate at the hands of their less well-endowed sisters."

"She attends informal social dos. We nod and say how do you do when we meet. You and your mother could call—I'm sure Mrs. Armstrong would be honored at the attention."

"The honor lessens, however, when she learns we've called to reclaim Ginger, *n'est-ce pas?*"

"Quite, and naturally you don't want to get off on the

wrong foot with the 'lovely black hair and long lashes.' This is an unaccustomed fit of shyness, Monty!''

"You are mistaken. My fear is that she is not a female Mama should call on."

"Then call on her yourself and leave your mother here."

Lady Monteith overheard the end of their talk and added her mite to it. "That is what I told him! Either you go and let me stay home with Howard, or I'll go and you stay home with him. I dread to leave him alone. The servants aren't safe with his chasing them. He got Jennie cornered this morning."

"We'll be back before he's arisen," Monty said. "I come to think the easiest approach to Mrs. Armstrong is to write her a note requesting the return of Ginger."

"I hope to take the cursed cat home with me before your uncle is up."

Mrs. Bright pondered a moment and said, "Then you must have your tea leaves read. That is a safe sort of semisocial visit."

"Good God!" Lady Monteith exclaimed. "Is she a fortune-teller?"

"She read the leaves—just for fun," Samantha explained. "She doesn't accept money for it."

"We'll do it, then," Lady Monteith decided, "and count on the weight of our titles to carry us through. I wish people would decide what class they are in. I don't know whether I am going on a social call or a business visit."

"Neither one nor the other," Monty said. "You are going on a pilgrimage, as one philosopher to another, seeking the truth regarding tall, dark strangers and trips and letters en route to you. In short, you are having your leaves read. Why don't you come with us, ladies?" he said to the Brights.

"Three readings will take too long," his mother objected. "Put down your cup, Monty. We must get the cursed cat and dash back to the Hall. I have some hope

38

Howard will spend the day in bed. He wanted only cold lemon water for breakfast—which didn't keep him from chasing Jennie.''

"And catching her," Monteith added. "Fortunately, I was close at hand for the rescue."

"With luck, his dyspepsia is worsening," Lady Monteith said. "I wonder what is good for it."

"Warm milk and bread, I should think. Papa always took pap," Samantha suggested.

"She means good for making it worse," Monteith explained. "A quick demise is your goal, is it not, Mama?"

"I don't wish the man ill, but it would make life a deal easier for the rest of us if he could be confined to his bed."

Lady Monteith straightened her furs around her shoulders and they left. The Brights went about their customary chores. Mrs. Bright was with her housekeeper scanning the shopping list and Samantha was in the kitchen, in hands with the lace collars from her gowns. These she always washed herself, as it was a fussy and time-consuming job. Her mind wandered to the unusual advent of Lord Howard into the daily life of Lambrook. It was amusing to see Lady Monteith scramble for anyone. She would have her hands full trying to manage the nabob. What a quiz he was, she thought, and smiled at the memory of his brandishing the scimitar with a sword clamped between his teeth. He was really quite handsome and dashing. She hoped he wasn't confined to his bed for too long.

Wrapped up in thought, she didn't notice the butler approaching her. "You have company upstairs, Miss Bright," he said, causing her to start in surprise.

"This early? Is it the Monteiths come back?" she asked.

"No, ma'am. The gentleman is Lord Howard."

"Lord Howard!" She stared, eyes blinking. "What on earth is he doing here? It's only ten o'clock! And he's supposed to be ill."

"He looks in fine fettle, ma'am," the butler said, with a twinkle in his eyes, for the servants were well aware of what was going on in the neighborhood. "He particularly asked to see yourself."

"Oh, dear!" she gasped. Her hands flew to her hair in a preening gesture not used for gentlemen of no interest. She removed her apron, wiped her hands, and went upstairs.

The booming accents of Lord Howard were audible from the end of the hallway. "The lemon water set me back up on my pegs in jig time. I was a little surprised to hear Irene and Monteith had come calling on you so early. I decided to add myself to the party."

Samantha hastened to the doorway and looked in. The dyspepsia left no trace of weariness on their caller. He was obviously not a young man, but he was also not approaching anything like decrepitude. Energy emanated from him like heat from a winter grate, and his toilette was in the highest kick of fashion.

She smiled and went in. "Good morning, Lord Howard. This is a surprise. I'm happy to see you've recovered."

He rose punctiliously and bowed. "Recover is the wrong word entirely. I was not ill. I haven't been bedridden since the turn of the century. I had a bad fit of dysentery in the tropics, but that is long past." He thumped his chest playfully. "I am in the prime of life, missie. Come and sit beside me. Your mama was just telling me you ain't engaged or anything of that sort. The gentlemen hereabouts must be a slow bunch of tops."

Samantha felt a rush of pleasure at his warm compliments. "No, I'm not engaged," she said.

"I am happy to hear it. Why go to London chasing after a Mrs. when there are prettier birds in Lambrook than ever flew out of it?" He drew Samantha onto the sofa beside him, while her mother looked on in futile dismay.

Samantha felt a strong inclination to laugh aloud, but confined the urge to a low gurgle in her throat. Good gracious, he's come *courting*! she thought.

"Your late papa was a colonel, as I recall?" he said.

"Yes, in the Dragoons."

"I remember young Bright. Brightie we used to call him. You have got something of his laughing eyes, missie."

That her suitor should call her father "young Bright" was a shock. She looked to her mother and said, "I am thought to take after my papa. Mama, you can see, is a mere slip of a thing compared to me."

"I like a good strapping lady." He nodded approvingly.

Mrs. Bright hardly knew how to register her disapproval. The man was a Monteith after all, the brother-in-law of her best friend. Obviously she couldn't be rude to him, yet she wished to tell him in no uncertain terms that she disapproved of his behavior toward her daughter.

"My daughter is twenty-six, Lord Howard. I believe it was mentioned last night."

"I'm aware of that, madam. You are thinking I am a bit long in the tooth for her, and she is a bit young for me, but I assure you she can handle me. I'm not the sort to cut up rusty with a young wife and beat her into submission. I appreciate your concerns. What do you know of me, after my having spent decades abroad amongst heathens? But this is only a friendly visit. My greatest fault is that I say what I should only think. A man can't help thinking."

"It is your views on suttee that concern me!" the worried mother exclaimed.

He laid his head back on the sofa cushion and laughed merrily. His teeth, she noticed, were in excellent repair. His open mouth reminded her of a picture of a crocodile. Then he lifted his head and turned serious. "Let me lay your fears to rest on that score at once. That is merely my personal feeling about a custom carried on in a foreign country. It wouldn't do in England. I wouldn't expect my widow to hop into the flames. It stands to reason no lady who had just come into a million pounds would want to

41

burn before she had a chance to spend it. As to my religion, it may relieve your mind to know that my next social call this morning is on the reverend and his lady. I mean to toe the line very properly.''

Samantha bit her lip and quietly studied their caller. She found him interesting—fascinating—but hardly as a husband. "We are happy to have you visit as a friend," she said. "It may be premature to—"

He lifted a hand and silenced her. "Say no more. I have jumped in too quickly. Blame it on my impetuous youth," he said, laughing. "It was poorly done of me to start hinting at my intentions so early in the game. You must get to know me first, and I must get to know you. It may well turn out we boil at different degrees. I haven't had a good look around yet myself, for that matter. But I usually know what I want, and as soon as ever you looked at me with those big, bright eyes, I said to myself, 'You'll not do better than that little lady, Howard my lad. Not if you look for a century.' I daresay I didn't make that strong an impression on you. I'm not much to look at, with my hide tanned like a saddle, but I'm a gentleman beneath the leather, and a richer one than you're likely to meet this side of the ocean. My wandering ways would cease once I was shackled to a good wife. She would want for nothing that love or money could buy."

He picked up her hand and held it a moment. Samantha looked at his strong brown fingers holding hers. She was strangely affected by his blunt speech, and didn't want to hurt him. Nor did she feel at all physically repelled by Lord Howard. He was still virile and attractive. How old was he anyway? He was the late Lord Monteith's younger brother. He might be younger than she had been thinking. Partis were few and far between in Lambrook. She was already twenty-six; all of her girlfriends were married.

Lord Howard chuckled. "Here am I pushing my suit forward again at top speed, when I have just promised you I would slow down. You make me lose control of my feelings. But there is no harm in it—your mama is here to see I don't step out of line.''

Mrs. Bright coughed discreetly. She, too, found something oddly attractive in his straightforward manner and the energy of his affection. Samantha gently withdrew her fingers, and an embarrassing silence fell on the company. It was broken by the sound of the door knocker, quickly followed by Lord Monteith's voice.

Almost before Samantha had time to think, the Monteiths were in the saloon, their eyes large in astonishment. Monteith lifted a quizzical brow at Sam.

''Howard, what the deuce are you doing here?'' Lady Monteith demanded, like a scolding mother.

Howard rose politely and smiled. ''I came down to join you. The servants told me where you were.''

''But you're supposed to be ill!''

''Devil a bit of it. The sight of Miss Bright is enough to cure a leper. How does it happen I got here before you? You left home half an hour ago.''

The Monteiths were seated, and the conversation resumed. From his chair facing Samantha, Lord Monteith studied her closely. Now why was Miss Rusticity smirking like the cat who just swallowed the cream? A blush was flattering to the lady. His eyes moved to Lord Howard. He, too, looked a trifle discomposed. Was it possible the old gaffer had come on a courting expedition? His lips worked unsteadily when he caught Samantha's eye.

''I went to have my fortune told,'' Lady Monteith said.

''Was Mrs. Armstrong at home?'' Mrs. Bright asked, as the visit had been short.

''She was still in bed, if you please! We were invited to wait, but were too anxious—'' A guilty glance toward Lord Howard betrayed the cause of her anxiety. ''I was wondering, Samantha,'' Lady Monteith continued, ''if you would mind speaking to Mrs. Armstrong—about that matter we discussed recently.''

Lord Howard listened with interest. ''The morning is

still young," he said. "Why don't we wait an hour and all go to the fortune teller? I don't believe a word they have to say, but it is good, innocent fun. Does your vicar disapprove of it?" he asked the company at large.

"What business is it of his?" Lady Monteith snipped.

Lord Howard thought a moment before replying. "He seemed the sort who made things his business. I've just been telling Miss Bright I mean to call on him this morning. A new organ or stained glass window will get me in solid in that quarter. I'll nip over and say how do you do, then we'll all meet here and go on to the fortune teller. Does that suit you all?"

"No, it does not," Lady Monteith said firmly. "I think you ought to go home to bed, Howard." An organ would cost a fortune!

"Nay, I have business to tend to. You run along, if you're in a yank to get home, Irene."

Lady Monteith sat, uncertain what was the least objectionable course, and finally took her decision. Monteith would accompany his uncle, and she would return to rearrange the household to Howard's comfort. The guests left together and went their different ways.

Mrs. Bright fanned herself with a magazine and said, "It looks like the beginning of a very strange summer, does it not?"

"Uniquely strange," Samantha agreed, and laughed. "How am I to handle Lord Howard if he persists in this farouche notion of courting me?"

"You must show him from the beginning that you are not interested, Samantha. I don't think you should have let him hold your hand."

"But perhaps I am interested—a little," her daughter said pensively. "He's really quite amusing."

"Irene will be in the boughs."

"Oh, that doesn't bother me, Mama," Samantha said pertly. "I would enjoy to pester her a little."

Mrs. Bright pinched her lip, and when she looked up,

44

a mischievous smile lurked in her eyes. "It would serve her right! Irene has held sway in the village for too long."

"Sending me off to recover the stuffed cat, as though I were a footman! I don't believe I shall do it. Why should I?"

"Because she is our friend, and she needs our help," her mother replied simply.

"No, I shall go because I want to," Samantha decided. "And I shall have my fortune told while I am about it. Will you come with me?"

"One of us should stay home in case callers come. There will be a spate of callers this morning to hear all about Lord Howard."

"I shan't be long."

Samantha got her bonnet and pelisse and was off.

Chapter 6

Mrs. Armstrong was up and dressed and extremely curious by the time Samantha reached her door. Like everyone else in the village, Mrs. Armstrong knew of Lord Howard's arrival home. Like most, she knew from her servants that Monteith's carriage had stopped at Bright's door, followed shortly by Lord Howard's, knew to a fare-thee-well that the nabob was presently ensconced in the vicar's house with Lord Monteith. All very interesting to be sure, but how had *she* become involved? First, Lord Monteith and his mama calling on her, now Miss Bright. Some vague thought of fortune-telling was at the back of her mind. A gentleman just returned from India might conceivably have some interest in the occult. What never occurred to her for an instant was the mangy old cat stuck up in the attic.

Mrs. Armstrong was elated by her sudden surge in popularity. She had played a careful game when establishing herself in Lambrook. It had been necessary to vacate other out-of-the-way homes due to a too hasty making of friends—the wrong kind of friends. She was retired from her real business now. At thirty-five, a woman with thirty thousand in the bank didn't have to entertain any gentleman she didn't care for. The little trouble with Mrs. Armstrong was that she cared for most gentlemen. But in Lambrook she had been as careful as a nun. No one guessed her seamy past, and she intended to settle down as a respectable matron. When she was sure she liked Lambrook and Lambrook liked her, she'd send home and have Jimmie join her. Her son would be raised like real gentry. And if some respectable, well-to-do gent wanted to make her an offer of marriage, she might consider it.

Meanwhile, she would go below and see what high-and-mighty Miss Bright had to say for herself. All Mrs. Armstrong's gaudier gowns were stored in a trunk at her mother's house. What she had bought to wear in Lambrook were what she considered dully respectable outfits, enlivened only by her own considerable charms. A mauve morning gown with a fichu right up to her collarbone was relieved from monotony by the close cut that showed clearly the line of her bosoms. Her jet hair was saved from dullness by a gold butterfly tucked into her curls. She was too old for ribbons, and though ostensibly a widow (as a spinster disliked to claim a son), she was too lively for caps.

As she entered her saloon, her dark eyes were alive with curiosity. Samantha gazed and found herself still unable to put Mrs. Armstrong into a recognizable category. With all the outward trappings of gentility, there was something about her that didn't sit right.

"Good morning, Mrs. Armstrong." She smiled uncertainly.

Mrs. Armstrong had no intention of recognizing her caller, and pinned a curious smile on her handsome face. "Good morning, madam. You wished to see me?"

"Yes, I'm your neighbor from across the street—Miss Bright."

"Ah! And you've come for a reading?"

"Yes."

Mrs. Armstrong gave a polite little *tsk* of annoyance. "What foolish lady gave you the idea I make a career of that nonsense? I only do it for amusement amongst friends." Though her words were harsh, she smiled pleasantly and took up a chair, to prevent her caller from rising. "But now that you are here, we shall have tea, and if you like, I'll glance at the leaves. I'll ring for my servant."

The tea was sent for, and Mrs. Armstrong waited. Samantha shifted uneasily in her chair. She had never felt so uncomfortable in her life. Mrs. Armstrong made a strong impression on everyone she met. It was her eyes that did it, Samantha thought. They were clever, bright, beautiful eyes, long and dark and as cold as ice water.

"It's warm for this time of year," Samantha said.

"Yes."

After a little silence, Samantha decided to forge ahead with her real errand. "It was Lady Monteith who asked me to call. She accidentally gave something to the church bazaar—an item she wishes to recover. It was a stuffed cat—a brindle cat with glass eyes. I believe you bought it?"

Mrs. Armstrong had bought the cat to show the village she was willing to do her bit for charity. She had no more use for it than anyone else, but she thought it might amuse Jimmie. Meanwhile, it sat in its glass case in the attic gathering dust.

"Good gracious." Mrs. Armstrong laughed. "That was months ago. Why does she suddenly want it now?" The name Lord Howard was in her mind, and the possibility that those green eyes were valuable—emeralds perhaps. They must take her for a simpleton!

"It actually belonged to Lady Monteith's brother-in-law. He has returned from India and has expressed an interest in it," Samantha explained. "It's quite valueless, and as I see you aren't using it as an ornament, I thought perhaps you wouldn't mind selling it back. Naturally, I'd reimburse you."

Mrs. Armstrong waved the idea of reimbursment away with a careless hand. "I would be delighted to return it if I had it." She smiled. "I don't believe I kept the thing. I picked it up on impulse—one wants to contribute something to the bazaar—but I didn't keep it.''

"Do you remember who you gave it to?''

Mrs. Armstrong laid a dainty finger against her cheek and pondered. "It may come to me. I'll try to remember, Miss Bright.''

"It's rather urgent, actually. Would the servants know?''

Mrs. Armstrong's dark eyes narrowed suspiciously. Rather urgent, was it? The thing must be worth a fortune. It could be stuffed with diamonds, for all she knew. "I'm afraid not. I shall put on my thinking cap and try to recall. That was the week I sent a parcel of old clothes and things to a charity house I sponsor in London.'' Little was known of Mrs. Armstrong, but it was known she came from London.

"Ah, here is our tea!'' the hostess exclaimed, and smiled. The subject of the cat was forgotten.

Samantha drank up her tea rather hastily. Mrs. Armstrong was just discovering in the leaves a tall, dark, elderly gentleman who had come from a distant land (for she was eager to talk about Lord Howard) when the door knocker sounded.

Within seconds, Lord Monteith and Lord Howard were shown into the little saloon. Samantha watched with amazement as Mrs. Armstrong's expression shifted. Her polite smile didn't widen. It was the eyes that changed. The lids drooped somewhat, and a more gentle look came over the hostess. Her whole body posture became softer, and when she spoke, her voice had turned playful.

"I am honored to receive two such distinguished visitors,'' she said. Her eyes hardly knew which to honor as she spoke, but common sense told her Monteith was above her touch, while the noble blackamoor was quite in her style. Raffish, rich, old, and lecherous. She saw the glint of interest in Lord Howard's eyes and studied him from

49

under demure eyelids. "I was just reading Miss Bright's leaves," she said and smiled. "You must forgive the foolish fancy of we ladies."

Greetings were exchanged again with Samantha, then Lord Howard turned his attention to the hostess.

"Foolish is what it is," he agreed. "I am all for foolishness myself, so long as it don't break the bank. Not that I mean to say we don't intend to pay! We have come for a reading, madam, if you will be so kind."

Mrs. Armstrong waved the mention of payment aside with the same smile that greeted Samantha's suggestion of paying for the cat. It was obviously the cat that had brought Lord Howard to her door, but she'd let him bring up the subject. Her estimate of the ugly thing's value soared through the roof. She could hardly wait to get up to the attic and rip it apart to learn its secret.

"It is only a hobby, but I will be happy to oblige you, gentlemen."

She sent for more cups and poured the tea. "Now you must not add milk. Just drink it up, leaving a few drops in the bottom to swirl the leaves. Who will go first?"

Lord Howard never took second position. "You can start with me," he said.

"Shall we just remove a bit to the corner? Peace and quiet are necessary for a proper reading." She led him off to the other side of the room.

"This sofa will be comfortable," she decided. The diffused light filtering through the curtains was also flattering. As she spoke, Mrs. Armstrong moved to Lord Howard's side, and he began some brusque flirtation. Monteith turned to Samantha and winked.

"Why did you bring him here? She might mention the cat," Samantha said in a quiet aside.

"Did you ever try to stop a tornado? He was coming, with or without me. Has she got it?"

"No, I think she gave it away to some charity in London. She's bound to mention it. I didn't intimate it was a secret.''

Mrs. Armstrong turned a knowing eye to the whispering couple. "You must drink up your tea, Lord Monteith," she chided.

Lord Howard's cup rattled in his saucer and he proclaimed himself ready. "I hope you see a pretty lady in the logs and leaves," he said, handing the cup to Mrs. Armstrong. "You would certainly see one if you looked in your mirror.''

"You are too kind." She took the cup and held it aloft, the better to show off her well-shaped arm. "The type of cup used is important," she said. "It mustn't have any pattern inside, to confuse the arrangement of the leaves. It shouldn't have ridges or be too narrow at the bottom. This is the right sort of cup—oh, but you've left too much tea, Lord Howard. We only want half a teaspoon. You must sip a little more." She held the cup to his lips. Lord Howard gazed deeply into her eyes as he slowly sipped, taking care not to make a racket.

When the proper amount of tea remained, she said, "I see you are right-handed. You must hold the cup by the handle and swirl it quickly." Lord Howard gave it a swirl. "No, not like that! Counterclockwise." Again, her dainty white fingers touched his hand, guiding it in the proper course. "You get a wish," she said in her gentle voice. Her dark eyes gazed into his. "Just wish for what you want.''

Their eyes held over the moving cup. Lord Howard was struck most forcibly with the notion that the young female was not averse to fulfilling his every wish. A pity Miss Bright should be present, or the thing could be settled on the spot.

"Now turn the cup upside down on the saucer," she ordered. "Place your left hand on the bottom of the cup—like so." Again, her fingers guided his with loving touch. "And the right hand on top of the left. Now you concen-

51

trate on your wish." Her body inclined to his as she spoke, just as he wished.

He glanced impatiently to Monteith and Miss Bright, who were engaged in some private conversation. "A complete reading ought to be done in private, I expect," he said.

She lifted her dark eyes and gazed at him. "That would be best, if you're serious about learning your future, Lord Howard. I thought it was only an idle pastime?" The intensity of her gaze went far beyond reading leaves, and they both knew it.

"I'll come back this evening," he whispered. "Say about nine? Just make up anything you like for now."

Mrs. Armstrong spouted a deal of nonsense about seeing the cup's interior as a clock, each number having to do with direction, each level from rim to bottom designating a stage of the future as well.

"An archway, Lord Howard! That is a sign of hope! And look at all the little dots—that signifies money. You are going to come into money."

"Look at the time zone again, missie. I already have money. Plenty of it. Do you see a lady in the near future? That is what interests me!"

"I see a gate," she said, with another long look. "That means an opportunity awaits."

"Excellent! Does the position indicate nine this evening?"

She lifted her chin, and her soft expression congealed in annoyance. "Not quite so soon as that."

"There ought to be something in there to show jewelry," he tempted. "Do you see a bracelet or brooch? Ruby or emerald—anything you fancy."

The only item Mrs. Armstrong fancied was a golden band. She had no intention of sinking into her old occupation. She gave him a wounded look and set the cup down. "I have already told you, I don't accept payment

52

for reading the leaves," she said stiffly; then she beckoned Monteith forward for his reading.

His reading was much more businesslike. There was no touching of the hands, no long gazing into his eyes, though she was careful to discover bells and other signals of good fortune. As it had been hinted that money was not welcome, the gentlemen were at something of a loss as to recompensing their hostess.

"I hope we may have the pleasure of your company at the fête champêtre next week," Monteith said. "It will be held on the grounds of Lambrook Hall."

This charity affair was open to all and sundry without benefit of an invitation, but Mrs. Armstrong thanked her guest very civilly and bowed them all out. Then she raced up to the attic and began examining the cat. She knew a glass eye when she saw one, and she saw two plain glass eyes staring at her from the corner. They couldn't possibly be emeralds. Black dye had been melted into the glass. She snipped the taxidermist's stitches along the stomach and poured sawdust out onto the floor. There wasn't a thing in it—no diamonds, nothing. All the cat was good for was doing Lady Monteith a favor, and as it never did any harm to be on terms with the village's leading lady, she would stuff the sawdust back inside and restitch the horrid thing.

The morning was far from over. High Street was just coming alive when the party left Mrs. Armstrong's house.

"Shall we go for a little drive?" Monteith suggested.

"I'll take my morning constitutional," Lord Howard decided. "I want to walk up and down High Street and say good day to everyone. I have many old acquaintances to resurrect. There's no point your wasting your time, Monteith. Give me an hour or so and meet you at the inn. As Irene took your carriage home, you will have to go back with me."

Monteith deemed his uncle safe for an hour on High

Street and suggested Samantha go for a drive with him to pass the time.

"I'm surprised she didn't mention the cat," was Samantha's first speech once they were alone.

"I was on nettles, waiting for her to blurt it out. Mrs. Armstrong is a handsome woman."

"Woman, or lady? I still can't make up my mind."

"That would be due to your lack of intimacy with the former. Mrs. Armstrong is a handsome female, and a clever one, too. You notice I was allowed to arrange the leaves myself. Uncle required assistance at every turn. I think the old slice is after her."

"I think your nose is out of joint, milord. Howard has mighty broad taste if he cares for her. Not an hour ago he all but asked for permission to court me!"

Monteith stifled his amusement as long as he could, but soon a loud bark of laughter broke out. "You aim too high, miss! Don't mistake Uncle's Indian manners for romance. It will be an incomparable for him—if Mama and I don't prevent it."

Samantha felt a surge of anger at his laughing disbelief.

Monteith realized he had been gauche and tried to butter her up. "I daresay you are called an incomparable in the village."

"Yes, here amidst the stiff competition of Mrs. Jenkins and Mrs. Tucker, I have been called an incomparable; and two gigs are called heavy traffic."

"I'm sorry if I trod on your toes, but pray don't go calling a few meaningless compliments an offer of marriage."

"It might interest you to know the words 'pushing my suit forward' were used, and 'young wife'. It was *marriage* he was discussing, nothing else. He'd never marry Mrs. Armstrong—a widow. You know his views about that."

Monteith's laughter faded, to be replaced by a blank stare. "By God, I think you're serious!"

"What if I am? What's wrong with that?"

"He's twice your age!"

"I repeat, what's wrong with that? You're thirty-five. If you chose a deb of seventeen or eighteen, the world would smile in approval. I'm twenty-six—Howard can't be much more than fifty-two."

"He's fifty-five, more than a quarter of a century older than you. That's a good deal more than seventeen or eighteen years."

"It doesn't seem too much to me. The quarter of a century passed so far hasn't put many opportunities in my way. The next quarter could be much more interesting. Why shouldn't I have a taste of London society like everyone else? Balls and theaters and routs . . ."

"And the burra sahib accompanying you—when he's able."

"He's full of life. I never saw such an energetic man."

"You wouldn't say so if you'd seen him before he had his lemon water this morning. He looked green."

"He has amazing recuperative powers, then. He was all bright-eyed and bushy-tailed when he came calling on me."

Monteith scowled. Quite aside from seeing his uncle's fortune go out of the family, it was distasteful to think of his marrying a young girl like Sam. "What of his character?"

"I believe his assassinations will stop now that he's back in England."

"I was referring to his womanizing. Have you become so sophisticated you would countenance Howard's dangling after Mrs. Armstrong while courting you?"

She considered it a moment and answered with every appearance of seriousness, "No, if I decided to have him, I would insist he not visit Mrs. Armstrong. I would take up reading the leaves myself, if necessary."

"You'll have to take up more than reading the leaves.

That was a pretext for him to get a look at her. The next visit will entail more . . . intimate doings."

"I believe it was just a morning's amusement, no more."

"You deceive yourself. The thing to do is keep Uncle occupied," Monteith said, thinking aloud.

Samantha saw that already he had recovered from that first spurt of anger that Howard was interested in her. He didn't believe her—that was the fact of the matter. He didn't think she was pretty enough to have engaged his uncle's interest. She decided on the spot that she would not discourage Lord Howard's advances. She liked him; perhaps liking might grow into loving. And she'd show Monty that she was more than a simple country rustic, that other men appreciated her, even if he didn't.

"Perhaps I can help entertain him," she suggested, with a mischievous smile.

Monteith scowled and whipped up the horses. He turned the carriage around at the next corner and returned Miss Bright to her home, where she stormed in, wearing a heavy frown.

"What happened? Did you get the cat?" her mother asked eagerly.

"No, she's given it away. Monty and Lord Howard arrived and had their leaves read."

"Was Lord Howard very angry?"

"He doesn't know—about the cat, I mean."

"Then what has got you in a pelter?"

"Mrs. Armstrong is throwing her bonnet at Lord Howard."

"But what is that to you, Sam? Surely you aren't truly interested in him? He's older than your father!"

"Why shouldn't I be interested in a million pounds? Everyone else is!"

"Oh, Sam! Don't be ridiculous. He's not your type."

"There are many would jump at him. What *is* my type, Mama? Have I had a better suitor? No, I have had Mr.

Russel's assistant, and I have walked out twice with Mr. Pearson when he was visiting Clifford Sutton two years ago.''

"I always hoped you and Ted—"

"Ted doesn't seem to share your hopes. Since his graduation, we've hardly seen a sign of him. He's still a boy. Howard is a man. His wife will have a fascinating life, the sort of life you and I can hardly imagine. I would like to marry and have children, a home. . . ." A wistful sigh escaped Samantha's lips.

Her mother looked and nodded in understanding if not agreement. "You've had a narrow sort of a life," she said pensively.

"Narrow as a straw. Now the whole wheat field is opening before me, and all anyone can do is scold because I show some interest. I like Howard very much, Mama," she said mulishly, then ran upstairs before she should reveal what was really bothering her; that Monty had laughed out loud. That he didn't believe anyone was interested in her. She'd show him.

Mrs. Bright sat down to do serious battle with her conscience. Had she the right to try to dissuade Sam? Her daughter was eight years older than she was when she had married. Sam was grown up, and she was sensible. It would be fine to see her so well settled. Mrs. Bright's thoughts were so serious and sober that she didn't even think how the match would infuriate Irene. She decided that if Sam was sincerely attached to Lord Howard, she would do nothing to cast a rub in her way. But it would seem strange to have a son-in-law older than herself.

Chapter 7

Monteith kept his eyes and ears open when he joined his uncle later, to learn what, if anything, was said of Miss Bright. The first subject that arose was not Samantha, but Mrs. Armstrong.

"Would you know if the lady has a patron?" Lord Howard asked bluntly.

"I'm not aware that she has," Monty replied. "On the other hand, Uncle, you will hardly wish to take her under your protection at this time if you have in mind a more proper alliance. You mentioned marriage."

"One thing hasn't much to do with the other. My wife will be busy raising sons and running my house. A man requires his little diversions. You may be sure I would employ every discretion. Armstrong's location—just across the street from Brights'—is awkward. I daresay she has a back door."

The anger that clutched Monteith's heart was untinged with any monetary consideration. "Samantha's young enough to be your daughter," he said gruffly.

"A man don't marry a relict when he means to fill a nursery. Miss Bright has a good sturdy hip on her; she'll be a fine breeder. I look forward to it," he said, his eyes glowing lustfully.

Monteith's knuckles turned white. He dared not speak. It was all he could do to keep his hands from flying to

Howard's nose. All unaware, his uncle rattled on, "I want a wife young enough to tend to the kiddies after I am gone. There's no saying I'll see my lads fledged. I might very well stick my fork in the wall before they finish university. My intention, Monteith, is to make you my sons' guardian. I meant to mention it to you. You have no objection?"

"I have every objection!"

Lord Howard considered this a moment and put his own construction on it. "You will be pretty busy in the House, I daresay. It might be best to hire a brace of lawyers for the job."

From concern for his unborn sons, Lord Howard immediately reverted to his mistress-to-be. "About Mrs. Armstrong—I gather she is new in the village?"

"So I understand."

"I was wondering whether she is a real widow or a grass widow. I don't care much for getting tied up with the latter. You never know when their husbands will come pouncing home, spoiling for a fight. I have had some difficulty with husbands in the past. Now that I am home, I mean to keep my nose clean. I shall find out from her this evening."

"You're going to Armstrong's tonight?" Monty asked in alarm.

Lord Howard gave a knowing smile and said, "For a more thorough reading of the leaves. She suggested it herself. I wish I had thought to mention using the back door."

After a moment's pause, Monteith replied in very good spirits, "I doubt Miss Bright will be spying from her window. What time is your assignation?"

"Nine o'clock."

They continued on their way home. The afternoon passed with no major contretemps. Lord Howard was punctual for his reading that evening, and Mrs. Armstrong was more than punctual. She was ready and waiting half an hour before his arrival. Having had considerable experience with gentlemen of Lord Howard's kidney, she knew precisely what he was about, and was determined to turn the direction of his interest to more proper channels.

When he was shown in, she had arranged herself on the chaise longue in a romantically flowing garment that concealed all of her body except her head and arms. Her hair hung loose over her shoulders in black waves, and the lamps were low. The pose she had in mind was a sort of Delphic oracle of austere mystery and subtle refinement— a lady several feet above a gentleman's touch. The unattainable was what men liked.

To suggest she represented the divine rather than the profane, she had the table decked out as an altar, with votive candles and flowers. The wine decanter and glasses were on another table, to avoid jarring. As she had no notion of Lord Howard's aversion to marrying a widow, she meant to drop vague laments about her dear late husband, and possibly a tantalizing hint that she had foresworn any further romantic entanglements for the rest of her life. That should present him a tempting challenge.

When Lord Howard was shown in, he peered around the dark corners for his hostess till he espied the white form on the chaise longue. "Ah, there you are, Mrs. Armstrong. I hope I'm not barging in on a headache."

She lifted an arm in greeting. "In the evenings, I prefer the half light. It is more amenable to my mood."

Encouraged, he paced forward and grabbed her hand. He raised it to his lips and kissed it. Once this was done, however, he began to wonder just where he was to sit, as Mrs. Armstrong occupied the entire chaise.

"I shall ring for your tea," she said in a rather languorous voice.

"We'll skip the tea this evening, shall we?"

The expression she wore was one of innocent bafflement. "But I thought you came for a complete reading? Is it the palm you wish read?" she asked.

As this would at least get him onto the sofa, he said,

"That's it. I'll just slide in here beside you on the love-seat."

Mrs. Armstrong lowered her legs and patted the end of the chaise. She took Lord Howard's hand in both of hers and turned it palm-upward. She studied it a long moment, then closed her eyes and examined it with the tips of her fingers, slowly, seductively. The gentle, warm, insinuating pressure of her fingers fired Howard to such a state it was all he could do not to grab her into his arms.

When at last her eyes fluttered open, she gave a little surprised shudder. "Did you feel it, the emanation?" she asked.

"That I did, my dear. It shook me to the core."

"I have never felt such a strong emanation before. I believe our spirits are in tune. I shall begin the reading now."

She drew her index finger along the first line of his palm. "Ah, look at the length of the life line. You will live to ninety, Lord Howard." She continued with many portents of success and good fortune. "I have never seen such a large mount of the Sun! Success, intelligence, audacity."

"I can't deny the success at any rate. As to the audacity—" He laughed and tried to slip his arm around her waist.

Without a word or even a glance of rebuke, she removed the offending arm and proceeded with her reading. The mounts of Jupiter and Saturn and Mercury were all positive, but the mount that Lord Howard was interested in was unmentioned.

"What of my love life?" he asked archly. "The mount of Venus—you have not mentioned it."

"That, too, is satisfactory. I see love there, charity." Yet these virtues caused her lips to droop sadly. "Alas"—she sighed—"I also see much evidence of libertinage."

"It shows, does it?" he asked coyly, and decided it was time to get down to business.

He withdrew one of his many Indian jewels from his pocket and held in the palm of his hand a fine ruby ring. He slid it onto her finger and studied it a moment. "Plenty more where this one came from," he said, and tried once more to get his arm around her waist.

Mrs. Armstrong rose gracefully. "May I offer you a glass of wine, Lord Howard?"

"That would be dandy."

She poured wine, and when Lord Howard reached the bottom of his glass, he found the ruby ring there. "What's this?"

Mrs. Armstrong took a seat, not on the chaise longue but on a chair a few feet removed from it. "You are foolishly generous, Lord Howard," she chided gently.

"Damme, I wish you will call me Howard."

"Then you must call me Serena," she smiled, though her name was Nancy. "I don't accept payment for my readings. It is a gift I share with a few friends."

"I had hoped I might share another gift," he said, pinning her with an impatient eye.

Mrs. Armstrong just smiled sadly. "I shan't pretend to misunderstand your meaning. I am through with all that."

"Why, you're still in the prime of life! You can't be more than thirty-five."

"A little younger actually. Since my husband's death five years ago, I have forsaken the pleasures of the flesh, Howard. I leave that for more worldly creatures."

"Sure I couldn't tempt you?" he said, polishing the ruby ring.

"You could. That is why I must not see you again. Please, respect my wishes in this matter."

Her tactic worked splendidly. Lord Howard was quite smitten by her noble mien and that tantalizing weakness on her part. The lamplight flickering on her shapely arms and long, dark eyes imbued her with every allurement.

"I have been looking forward to this evening all day,"

he said, peering from the corner of his eye to read her reaction.

She reached across the intervening space and patted his hand. "I confess, I, too, have been tempted. But it would not do. I made a vow. . . ."

"What sort of vow?"

"When my husband was interred, I vowed on his grave that I would never remarry. Don't tempt me, Howard, I beg of you. I am only a weak woman, and you are strong. You might convince me to break my vow."

The word *remarry* set him back a peg. He had obviously misunderstood the lady's background. Pretty as she was, a lifelong commitment to a widow was still anathema to him. He put the ring in his pocket. Mrs. Armstrong lowered her long lashes and stared at her fingers. She made a very pretty picture, there in the flickering lamplight. By staring fixedly at the floor, she managed to raise a film of moisture that closely resembled unshed tears. Then she raised her eyes and smiled very sadly.

"Good-bye, dear Howard," she said. Her voice was uneven.

Lord Howard's fingers curled over the ruby in his pocket. It wasn't miserliness that kept the ring in his pocket, but respect. He didn't want to offend the poor lady.

"I'll be running along, then," he said.

At the doorway he stopped again and looked at Serena. Her head drooped on her shoulder like a wilted flower. She didn't mar her pose by looking up again. Lord Howard took away the proper vision of a chaste but troubled lady, cleaving to her vow—by no means sure she could go on cleaving if he persisted.

At Mrs. Armstrong's door, Howard looked carefully up and down the street before leaving. He glanced with particular interest to the lit windows of the Bright house. No head shadowed the clear rectangles of light, but he thought the door was opening and waved for his curricle. Had he looked as closely when he entered, he would have seen not one head but two.

Lord Monteith left Lambrook Hall half an hour before his uncle to pay an unexpected visit to the Brights. He and his mama were planning a round of social events to occupy Howard's time and divert his thoughts from marriage. An invitation to luncheon the next day was Monteith's excuse for calling, though not his reason. He also had another excuse.

"I've brought you a note from Mama," he said to Mrs. Bright as he handed her a letter.

Mrs. Bright read it and frowned. "Oh, dear, I'm not sure I want to be involved in this sort of havey-cavey going on."

"What is it, Mama?" Samantha asked.

"Irene wants to use our house to meet Clifford clandestinely. It seems Lord Howard has expressed himself with generous strength on the subject of widows' remarrying. She is afraid of offending him. I don't see that it is any of Lord Howard's business. He's only a brother-in-law."

"A very rich brother-in-law," Samantha added, with a challenging look to Monteith.

"The one who pays the piper calls the tune," Monty pointed out. "Mama cherishes the hope that he'll leave his fortune to Teddie and Bert."

Mrs. Bright shook her head. "Nothing ever comes of trying to butter up rich relatives, Monteith. My late husband curried favor with an old maiden aunt for years. He was always visiting her and sending her little gifts, and in the end she left everything to a second cousin who had the wisdom to ignore her entirely till the last few months, when he moved in and ingratiated himself. And he didn't need the money as badly as we, either."

"I agree with you," Monteith said. "Unfortunately, Mama doesn't agree with me. Of course I would be happy to see Teddie and Bert so well provided for. If you don't

64

wish Mama to use your house, you have only to tell me so, and I'll give her the message.''

"I don't like to refuse her," Mrs. Bright said. "Irene has never asked anything of me before. Why doesn't she arrange her meetings at Clifford's sisters' houses?''

"They live in the country, Mama," Samantha pointed out. "Lady Monteith often comes to the village—our house is more convenient for her. Closer to Clifford's home, too.''

"Then it is not the principle that deters you?" Monteith asked Mrs. Bright. "You don't actually object to her meeting Clifford without Uncle's knowledge?''

"She's not beholden to him. She may meet Clifford any time or anywhere she wants. Well, I suppose there's no harm in it. She's not a young deb after all. I'll write up an answer, Monteith, for you to take home. I shall also tell her I think she wastes her time catering to Lord Howard.''

She went to the desk in the corner and began composing her reply. Monteith gave Samantha the invitation to luncheon the next afternoon.

"Uncle plans to display some of the things he brought back from India," he mentioned, while she read it. "Carts are arriving at the door daily, ladened with goods. Enough swords to outfit the Dragoons, along with all manner of artworks. But the pièce de résistance is the jewelry. It will go into the bank vault soon, so this is your chance to see it.''

Samantha returned the invitation to the envelope. "You need not add any further enticement, Monty. A chance to meet Lord Howard is quite sufficient to lure me to the Hall. Mama and I shall be there.''

His dark eyes glinted and he said, "I thought perhaps you would prefer to remain home, learning how to read the leaves. That was your intention, was it not?''

"Only as a last resort if Mrs. Armstrong proves a serious competitor.''

65

Monteith glanced at the clock on the mantel. It read two minutes to nine. He rose and wandered idly to the window. "There's a carriage passing by," he said, and pulled the curtain aside a little to distinguish the carriage.

Samantha glanced out, too. "It's the vicar's gig," she said. "He drove over to his other parish this afternoon. He's interviewing a new assistant."

When Monteith remained at the window, Samantha became curious. "Are you thinking of setting up a gig, Monty? Or were you hoping for a glimpse of Mrs. Russel's new bonnet? She didn't accompany him."

"No, I believe I see another set of lights coming this way."

"Heavy traffic indeed! You will be thinking you're back in London, with such a plethora of carriages."

"It looks like Howard's curricle," Monty said casually.

Samantha cast a teasing smile at him. "As you are so frightened of offending the nabob, perhaps you had best leave. He might be annoyed to find you here when he comes courting me." She was gratified that Lord Howard should time his visit with Monty's. Excitement lent a rosy tinge to her cheeks and a sparkle to her eyes.

Monteith turned around. "Best order the tea, Sam. It looks as if you must begin learning to read the leaves."

Samantha's anger was at being thwarted in front of Monteith. Not only thwarted, but after having boasted in front of him. "Is he going to Armstrong's?" she asked, and ran to the window, just as Lord Howard descended.

Monty studied her quick flash of anger. His eyes narrowed visibly. "That gets your hackles up, I see! One dislikes to say I told you so, but I did intimate something of the sort, if you will recall."

"So you did. As worn-out clichés are the style this evening, I shall say 'It takes one to know one.' "

"One what?"

"One libertine," she snipped.

"But *I* am not calling on Mrs. Armstrong. I am much more decorously employed visiting friends."

"Decorous, my foot! You knew perfectly well Lord Howard was going there. That's the only reason you came."

"I came to deliver Mama's letter and the invitation."

"It's the first time you've honored us with this personal delivery service. A footman was always good enough before. You came to spy on Lord Howard and me. Why else have you been monitoring that window so assiduously? That's despicable behavior, Monteith!"

He studied her, a frown pleating his brow. "You really mean it! You're really angry that Howard isn't visiting you."

"I couldn't care less about that," she said, and flung herself impetuously on the sofa. "What angers me is your duplicity."

"At the risk of bethumping you with yet another cliché, 'Methinks the lady doth protest too much!' My ill behavior never raised a flush before. A lady must care about a gentleman before she honors him with her wrath. Howard is the gentleman you want, not I. Shall I cross the street and interrupt the tête-à-tête for you?"

"Don't do it on my account. I expect you only want an excuse to call on Mrs. Armstrong yourself, if the truth were known."

"Truth is a phantom—unknowable, but I don't need an excuse to call on a lovely neighbor."

"I expect you're implying Mama and I are not lovely then, as you found it necessary to dream up *two* excuses to call on us."

Monteith threw up his hands in dismay. "You mistake excuses with reasons. There's never any point arguing with an angry lady. When logic goes against her, she begins discovering an insult in every innocent comment. You are overwrought to see your rich suitor dangling after the widow."

"No, Monteith, I am overwrought to see you spying on me."

"I feel like a Greek messenger." He sighed, and went to pour himself a glass of wine. "I only delivered the bad news, and here am I receiving your fire. Hold it for Howard," he suggested, and held the bottle up with a questioning look.

Samantha knew she had been betrayed into bad manners and nodded her acceptance. Mrs. Bright finished her letter and joined them for a glass of wine.

"Did I hear you say Lord Howard is visiting Mrs. Armstrong this evening?" she asked Monteith.

"You did, madam, but if it annoys you, please remember I only brought the news. I didn't make it."

"If that's the sort of man this foolish daughter of mine is encouraging, we had best learn it sooner than later."

Monteith lifted a brow and studied Samantha. "Actually *encouraging* him, is she? I must be on my best behavior then, if Sam is going to become my rich aunt."

Mrs. Bright clamped her lips and nodded her head. "You will look rather ridiculous, Sam—aunt to Monteith and sister-in-law to Irene."

"Why, Mama, I have nothing against a connection to the Monteiths. You shouldn't say such a thing in front of Monty."

"You know that was not my meaning. She is only joking," she assured Monteith.

"I am accustomed to jokes that aren't funny," he answered blandly. "I spend much time at Court and in the House of Lords. This sort of behavior is in no way novel to me." His tight lips suggested it was the running after money that was more familiar to him.

"Exactly how old are you, Sam?" he asked.

"Twenty-six years and three months."

"Hardly at that age where you should be snatching at straws," Monteith suggested, with a quizzing look. "I always thought you and Teddie or Bert might make a match of it."

"I assure you neither Teddie, Bert, nor myself ever thought anything of the sort," Samantha told him. "And neither did you till your uncle returned. If you're planning to sacrifice one of your brothers to save Lord Howard from me, Monteith, you're wasting your time."

"You're making a cake of yourself, Samantha," her mother said, and drew out her embroidery frame.

The conversation turned to more civil matters, and after ten minutes, Monteith rose to take his leave.

"The butler's in the kitchen polishing the silver, Sam. Will you get Monty's hat for him?" her mother said.

Samantha followed Monty out. "With the greatest pleasure," she muttered under her breath.

"My coming brings you no pleasure, but it's almost worth it to have the joy of showing me the door, eh, Sam?" He smiled and pulled the open the door, just as Lord Howard was coming from Mrs. Armstrong's house.

She gave him a pert look. "You should have been a little more patient, Monty! If you could have endured our company five minutes longer, you would have been here for your uncle's visit. Now, of course, you can hardly come back in without losing face."

Lord Howard hopped into his curricle and shot past the house without even looking sideways.

Monteith grinned at his fuming hostess. "There must be another cliché to cover this situation," he said. "Something about counting chickens before they're hatched suggests itself."

Samantha reined in her temper and smiled brightly. "It was a very short visit, was it not? Hardly long enough to encompass what you suspected."

"It don't take long to set up the terms," he said, and clamped his curled beaver over his eye at a rakish angle. "And now I shall escape, before you pick up the umbrella and have at me."

As Sam made no move for the umbrella, he hesitated a moment. "Cheer up, Sam. He's not right for you, you know."

Her frayed nerves snapped. "Don't you dare pity me!" she exclaimed, and slammed the door.

Chapter 8

Lady Monteith had her first assignation with Mr. Sutton at Mrs. Bright's the next morning. All the ladies had made extra attempts at being fine, as ladies will do when a new gentleman is on the scene. Irene wore an elegant feathered bonnet and rouge, and came with her son to forestall Lord Howard's suspicion. The meeting was not held in private, for the lovers were past that age when passion played a large part in their relationship. They sat in the saloon with the Brights and Monteith, having a cup of tea and gossiping.

"Where is Lord Howard this morning, Irene?" Mr. Sutton asked.

"The burra sahib says he has business in town," she answered. "That is what all his servants call him. Banking, I expect, is his errand. I hope he stays for lunch. He has a servant in the kitchen destroying the food with curry powder and some wretched hot spices. Monty tells me he called on Mrs. Armstrong last night."

Mr. Sutton looked closely to see what this portended, and Irene spoke on. "We have still not absolutely determined whether she is a lady, but it is just as well your sisters didn't call on her. Howard didn't breathe a word of the visit to me, which tells me *his* estimate of her standing. He told Monty she has taken a vow of celibacy. What do you make of that?'' This was asked in a purely rhetorical spirit.

Clifford never knew what to think of social doings till either Lady Monteith or his sisters told him, and waited to hear more. "How did the subject of her celibacy arise? You don't discuss a milcher's probable yield if you aren't thinking of buying the cow. She is after an offer of marriage, no less. And here we were afraid he would only make her his mistress. She is a dangerous woman,'' Lady Monteith declared.

"But if she is sworn to celibacy . . .'' Clifford said, frowning.

"Pooh! She'd forget that vow fast enough if she could get him to the altar. It was her way of telling him she was not open to any *other* sort of offer.''

"He'll never marry a widow,'' Monteith said.

His mother looked somewhat relieved and said, ''That is our only hope. At breakfast this morning he expressed himself with great strength on the evils of widows' remarrying. It is the outside of enough to have that blackamoor ordering us all about in our own home.''

"What did he say?'' Mr. Sutton asked.

"A deal of mumbo jumbo stuff about reincarnation. Such unchristian beliefs the Hindus hold! The excuse for incinerating the widows has to do with their coming back to life in another body, so giving up one life doesn't matter. They go a rung higher toward nirvana if they disport themselves properly regarding suttee.''

With her anger providing him a clue, Clifford said, "Sounds a proper con game to me.''

"All a hum,'' Lady Monteith agreed. "He doesn't believe a word of it, or even pretend to, yet he will persist in thinking widows shouldn't remarry. And it's not only widows whose fate he would decide. He had words for bachelors as well. He asked Monty a dozen times why he wasn't married yet. I was half of a mind to tell him Monty was engaged to Samantha, but on top of all Howard's other absurdities, he has been making up to Sam on the side himself. Did you ever hear of such a thing?'' she asked, and laughed.

''Robbing the cradle, what?'' Clifford ventured.

All eyes turned to examine Samantha, till she felt like something on view at Bartholomew's Fair. ''I vacated the cradle more than two decades ago,'' she said tartly. She said no more, as she was uncertain whether Lord Howard was courting her. His not calling the night before had raised a doubt.

Monteith smiled at her pique and leaned close for a private word. ''You seem fretful this morning, child. Teething, perhaps?''

She tossed her head boldly. ''I am cutting my wisdom teeth.''

''About time, too!''

Lady Monteith spoke on. ''Monty has written up a batch of letters trying to reach Teddie and Bert and bring them home.''

Listening, Samantha thought she followed the lady's line of thought. If Lord Howard was interested in her, she must be disposed of by some other means. Teddie or Bert would be made to offer for her. She stiffened at this cavalier ordering of her life. Lady Monteith railed against burra sahib's efforts to run the world, but she was attempting the same thing herself.

The conversation turned to other matters. There were many amusing incidents about Lord Howard's Indian servants and the havoc they were creating at the Hall to be related.

''To see them slipping through the dark hallways in their bed sheets is enough to frighten you out of your wits,'' Lady Monteith said. ''They look like ghosts. And bad as the ghosts are, Howard is worse by a long shot. I have had to confine Jennie to the kitchen, for he is after her like a fox after a hare, and she as innocent as a babe. I put Millie on upstairs service. She is a meager scrap of a thing, you know, and walleyed besides, so I trust she will be safe. If all else fails, I shall teach the footmen how to make up the beds and wield a feather duster.''

Monteith watched Samantha as these stories were being related. "One can certainly pity his future wife, whoever she may be," he said blandly.

"He shan't have a wife," his mother snapped. "We have agreed to that, Monteith. Though, I must confess, his health is stouter than I hoped. The dyspepsia came to naught, despite my best efforts. He didn't even call for lemon water this morning. He mentioned a recurring fever, however. I have some hopes that as summer wears on, the heat may get to him."

Samantha said through thin lips, "Wouldn't your best chance of killing him be to expose him to cold drafts, Lady Monteith? Surely a gentleman just returned from the tropics isn't going to cave in to our paltry English summers.''

Lady Monteith took no umbrage at either the suggestion or the tone. "I believe you're right!" she exclaimed. "A capital idea, Samantha. How clever you are. Do you know, Monteith, it might not be a dead loss if he *did* marry Sam. He wouldn't last more than a decade, and then she could marry Teddie.''

Lord Monteith had the grace to blush at this suggestion. As he listened to his mother, attuned to how her words must strike an outsider, he began to fidget uncomfortably. "Would you like to go out for a drive, Sam?" he asked.

"Why?" she asked suspiciously.

"Do you want a reason, or an excuse?"

"Neither one is necessary," his mother said. "You children run along."

Monteith rose and took Sam's arm. "Get your dollie, and we'll go out and play," he said.

They were about to leave when the door knocker sounded. A loud "Holloa" from the front hall announced the arrival of Lord Howard, and immediately he was shown in, bristling with smiles and energy. The older members of the party wore the guilty faces of miscreants. Whether it was their recent conversation or being caught at romantic connivings, Samantha was unsure. She was in no doubt as to Lady Monteith's change of tone, however. The lady could hardly fawn on him enough.

"Dear Howard! Come and join Mrs. Bright and myself." She smiled. She ignored Clifford, as if he were a cushion on the sofa. "I was just telling Mrs. Bright how lively things are at the Hall since you came. Planting those mangosteen things in the conservatory. And his cook is going to make us a curry for dinner," she added, with every sign of enthusiasm.

"Good day, ladies. And Mr. Sutton, isn't it? I'll pass on your invitation this time, thankee. I just came to call on Miss Bright. Are you game for a run in my curricle, missie?"

Lady Monteith spoke up quickly. "Monteith was just about to take Miss Bright for a spin, Howard. You come and join us old folks."

"I've no taste for sitting on my haunches sipping tea on such a fine day. I'll join the youngsters instead," he replied, and with a bow all around, joined himself uninvited to the younger party.

"We'll take my rig," Lord Howard said, as Samantha put on her bonnet. Behind his back, she gave Monteith a challenging smile.

"Three will be crowded in the curricle. We'll take my carriage," Monteith countered.

Lord Howard took Sam's elbow and winked at her. "Who in his right mind would object to being crowded by this bright-eyed young filly? But on such a fine day as this, my dear, wouldn't you prefer the open rig?" he tempted.

"No, Lord Howard," she answered, "in fair weather or foul, I would always prefer to honor my social commitments, and I agreed to drive with Monteith before you came."

"I will have to look sharp next time and get here before him! Heh, heh, I like a lady with spirit. Lead on then, Monteith. We'll take a run down the coast road, if you've no objection. There is a parcel of land there I want to see. I have just been talking to Gerard, a land agent, about buying up a few *begahs*."

"I have to go north," Monteith said. His tone was pleasant but firm. "I wish to speak to my bailiff."

"Excellent. If you're going that way, then I'll take Miss Bright in my rig. Now before you object, lad, listen to your uncle. A business trip is no way to entertain a young lady. If cutting me out is what you have in your mind, you'll have to do better than that. It's no compliment to a lady to be asked to tag along and sit on her thumbs while you speak to your *sircar*."

"We don't have *sircars* in England, Uncle," Monteith said, his voice becoming thin. "I doubt a lady is long entertained by hearing a foreign language that is meaningless to her, either. As to a business outing being poor amusement, Miss Bright cannot have much interest in your buying a *begah*—whatever that may be."

"It is a third of an acre, sir. And I trust Miss Bright might have some interest in the particular acres I have in mind, as they will be her future home if I ask her to marry me."

It would be difficult to say who was more stunned, Monteith or Miss Bright. They both stared and gulped. Samantha recovered first. She was in high spirits to see Monteith topped, for once. It was as beneficial as a balm to have Lord Howard announce his intentions in no uncertain terms. She watched in fascination as Monteith's shock turned to rising anger. The white column of his neck changed to rose, and his lips were clamped tight in a prelude to exploding. Before he could flare into words, she spoke.

"No, Lord Howard! Only if I *accept* your offer. Here

in England the ladies still have something to say about their fate."

"You've caught me dead to rights there." He laughed.

"As we are scarcely acquainted, you have no business speaking of marriage. But I'm curious to see the land. I assume you're going to build a house?"

"No, missie. A castle. There's already a little house on the land, Gerard tells me."

"Why don't you come along, Monty?" Sam invited. "It won't take long."

It was borne in on Monteith that if Howard was planning to build a castle, it was of some interest to him to see where and hear more details. He swallowed his spleen and tried to smile.

"Very well, we'll all go."

"You're welcome to tag along," Lord Howard said.

Lord Monteith tagged along on the outing that was to have been his own private one, and which he had anticipated with some pleasure. He always enjoyed Sam's company. With Howard dangling after her, Monteith was taking a closer look. His uncle might not be the tip of the ton, but he was no fool, either. He knew a good thing when he saw it. With maturity, Sam had become more sure of herself, more interesting.

It was Lord Howard who held the carriage door for Samantha, and he who climbed in beside her, with a careless word to Monteith to give his driver the directions. "The Langford property," he added.

Monteith was too surprised to be offended at his uncle's manner. The Langford property comprised a thousand acres of prime farm land, and held not "a little house" but a fine stone mansion. He gave his driver the order and took his seat on the banquette across from the others. "The Langford property, eh?" he said leadingly. "That's a fine estate."

"I like the situation, there on the ocean," Lord Howard said. "It reminds me of Calcutta. I shall drop a few yachts in the water for us to play with. A *masulah* if the surf is rough, and a batch of *paunceways* for our guests. For myself, I like a catamaran better than anything. My tastes are simple.''

''I wish your language were,'' Monteith interjected, but he went unheeded.

''We shan't be able to go inside the house without Gerard,'' Lord Howard continued. He aimed all his conversation at Samantha, which amused her and annoyed Monteith. ''He has the keys, but we shall have a look at the outside. From what he tells me, it might do for a guest house, except that I want that location on the point for my castle.''

''Lord Howard, I've been in the Langfords' house, and it is beautiful!'' Samantha objected. ''You surely aren't speaking of tearing it down and starting from scratch.''

''I can build right over it and make it an anteroom if you've a fondness for the place.''

The drive along the shore road was beautiful in spring, with the sparkling ocean below and birds screaming in the blue sky above. They turned in at a pair of handsome iron gates and followed a curved road up a slight incline to the house. The stone mansion's lordly location added to its beauty. It stood three stories high, a house in perfect repair.

''It looks so lovely—it just suits the location,'' Samantha pointed out.

''You may keep it for a toy house, if you and I come to terms,'' the nabob told her.

Samantha ventured a quick glance at Monteith, expecting some ironical remarks about dolls or toys. He was staring at his uncle with an expression that would curdle cream.

''I'll build a higher mountain up above it and put the castle there,'' Lord Howard continued. ''Yes, that would be best. The hill is a little squat, now I think of it. We would be better off with more altitude. You see how obliging I am,'' he complimented himself.

"Yes, indeed,'' she said, speaking halfway between her companions, but catching Monteith's eye to throw his words in his face. "One won't have to pity your wife— whoever she may be. And I wish you will not speak as if it were settled between us, Lord Howard.''

"You might at least stop 'lording' me!'' Howard said playfully. "Call me burra sahib if you don't like to use my Christian name yet. In that way, I can call you Sammie.''

Lord Monteith gave a snort of disgust and managed to turn the conversation to pounds and pence. He learned what he feared—that his uncle had been quoted a price a good deal higher than the property was worth. "But I'll shake them down ten percent,'' Howard said. "Gerard tells me they are anxious to sell.''

The Langford house was untenanted, and they got down from the carriage to walk around it. While Monteith was taking a close look at the state of the house, Lord Howard got Samantha alone to point out the various views.

"The only thing holding me up in the purchase is the number of *begahs* that go with it,'' he said, frowning.

"You don't want to farm, I take it?''

"I'm past that, but even without farming, you see, three thousand *begahs* is only a thousand acres. A man likes to have a few more inches than that to spread out in. Gerard is approaching the folks on the west side to see if they're interested in selling some land. If they are agreeable, I might close. So what do you think, Sammie?''

"I think you are very extravagant, sir!''

"And old bleater like me has to be a bit extravagant to land himself a prime young creature. I know Monteith has a prettier face and a less hagged one. I didn't know he had you in his eye, though I should have known if I'd thought about it. I wouldn't like to butt in if he is on the edge of offering for you. I'm all in favor of seeing the young bucks settle down. I had the notion it was young Teddie that fancied you. I figured I had a good chance against a younger son.''

''None of them fancies me, Howard. We are just friends. And are you quite sure *you* don't fancy someone else more?''

''No one I've seen so far.''

She looked him in the eye and said, ''I thought perhaps Mrs. Armstrong appealed to you.''

''There is nothing for me there. She ain't the sort of gel I took her for.''

This admission of philandering was given without a blush, and so were the lies that followed it. ''Don't think anything of that sort would continue after I was married,'' he assured her. ''I'd be constant as the North Star.''

Before she had to reply, Lord Monteith joined them. And she was glad not to have to make any decision yet. In twenty-six years, no gentleman she liked any better than Lord Howard had offered for her. Despite his age and despite his peculiar manners, he was attractive. His incredible wealth imbued him with an aura that made manners unnecessary. He was extravagant and interesting and even handsome, to a certain extent. How much was she allowing her petty annoyance with Monteith and his mother to color her thinking? It would be folly to marry from spite. Or was it his fortune that lured her? To speak of ''dropping a few yachts in the river'' appealed to her. Though not poor, the Brights had never been rich in the way the Monteiths were rich.

A whole new world would be opened to her. Travel, society, living in a castle. But living with Lord Howard— who would soon be an old man.

As if reading her thoughts, Lord Howard suggested he and Monteith take a dart down to look at the water. The path led down a rocky cliff, which he executed with the agility of a mountain goat. Coming up, which was a deal harder, left him still unwinded. He was no more tired than Monteith.

"The ladies might find the climb a little arduous," he said to Samantha. "It would be no trouble to have a staircase chiseled into the rock face, or an iron set of stairs put in."

Monteith looked across the water, thinking. This lavish-handed way of living must appeal to someone like Sam, who had never been beyond Lambrook, except for a few trips to London. And why should that anger him? He knew his mother was foolish to think she could bear-lead the nabob. He would surely marry some young lady. Why not Sam? He looked over his shoulder and found her gazing at him.

"We should be leaving if we want to get home in time for luncheon," he said.

Chapter 9

Lunch at Lambrook Hall held a few surprises for Samantha. The size and quantity of the jewels on view were not amongst them. After hearing Lord Howard's views on a house, she expected the jewelry to be plentiful and ostentatious. She found that rubies and emeralds and even diamonds could be tiresome when they covered the surface of a whole table. Many of the stones had not been set yet and were held in little leather pouches. Those that had been mounted were poorly done and reminded her of the tawdry paste jewels seen in the village "everything" shop.

After the guests had said "Very nice," and "How lovely," and "I didn't know emeralds-rubies-diamonds came in such a large size" half a dozen times, they ran out of compliments. It was for Lord Howard himself to show them the way.

"This little gem was given me by the nawab of Sutani." He smiled, holding up an ugly length of diamond chain. "It is to be worn on the ankle. Every gem is perfect. Not a flaw in them, a diamond merchant told me. You'll never guess what I got it for." He looked around expectantly, but no one was willing to hazard a guess.

"For taking the nawab's measurements and ordering him a jacket from London," he said, and laughed raucously. "I was the nawab's head man for a few years. Clerking didn't pay worth a tinker's curse. Any gentleman with his wits about him dropped it after a month. I gave it up as soon as I found where the real blunt was to be made. Come and try it on, missie," he said, holding the piece out to Mrs. Tucker, and using it for an excuse to leer at her ankles. The Sutton ladies and their husbands had been beckoned to the affair, though Clifford was excluded.

Mrs. Tucker emitted a shocked croak and recoiled in horror. "On your arm then, if you're shy," Lord Howard said, and hung it on her wrist.

Lady Monteith took the notion he might be planning to give each lady guest a gift, and quickly snatched it back. Over a peculiar luncheon at which each dish was heavily spiced and odd tasting, Lord Howard drank a good deal of wine and regaled them with details of his variegated career in India. He had apparently offered his talents to assorted highly placed Indian princes whose aim in life was to ape English manners.

"I must have ordered more silver and china from England than the whole royal family put together. I got a cut of ten percent from Rundell and Bridges when they discovered what I was about, raised the price by five hundred percent plus shipping when I sold it, and still got a hefty bonus from the nawabs for each purchase. It is a license to make money, being a nawab's man. They have more blunt than they know what to do with."

"They'd do better to spend some of it on their people," Monteith said. "From what you've said before, the lower class lives in dire poverty."

"They're used to it. What can you do with people who go on breeding like rabbits and won't eat beef?" he replied.

"Perhaps that is why they practice that dreadful suttee," Mrs. Bright said. "To control the population."

"Damme, it has nothing to do with that," Lord Howard corrected her. His face was flushed and his eyes glazed, but he filled his glass again and continued. "It has to do with propriety. No man of taste would eat another man's leftovers. I'll be dashed if he should—"

"*Do* try some of this lovely chutney on your meat, Howard," Lady Monteith said rather quickly, and passed the dish along. "So tasty. I must get the recipe from Suwani."

"I'll have him mix up a batch for you. It has fruit and lemon and seasonings and spices. Try a little, Irene. You'll find it makes even this tame ragout edible."

Lady Monteith put a dab on the farthest edge of her plate, and Lord Howard was off on another spiel of having outwitted a prince.

"Well, ladies, you must excuse me," Lord Howard said when lunch was over. "I still have the Indian habit of taking a snooze in the heat of the day, though I'm getting over it. The noonday sun was like the blast from a furnace. And myriad mosquitoes! They come in clouds to carry off your blood." Shortly after he left the room, the high-pitched squeal of a servant girl under attack was heard.

It was obvious to everyone that the nabob was more than ready for bed. How he had drunk two bottles of wine and still stayed on his feet was close to a miracle. The company smiled politely and settled in to discuss affairs. Samantha was relieved to get away when Monteith suggested a walk through the park.

"I think your mother might have included Mr. Sutton without arousing Howard's suspicions," she said idly.

"That is one good effect of Uncle's visit," Monty countered. "I wouldn't be sorry to see a little cooling in that quarter."

"I didn't know you had anything against the match!"

"I am not so outspoken as Uncle, but there are some few ladies a man is reluctant to see in the hands of another man. His mother, sisters—you," he added, with a quizzing little smile, and took hold of her fingers. Monteith had often held Samantha's elbow; it was the first time her fingers had been so honored. This intimate touch made her feel self-conscious.

"Why me? You've never treated me like a sister."

"Haven't I ignored you assiduously all these years? That is how siblings treat one another, unless one of them is in trouble, in which case we rally to the defense. I am exerting every effort to herd Teddie and Bert home to make their overtures to Uncle. And I intend to protect your gentle self from his invasions as well."

"If I were your sister, you'd be pitching me at his head."

"No, Mama would."

"It's your house. You're the head of the family. But pray don't feel it necessary to protect me from a million pounds!"

"A billion pounds wouldn't make that yahoo palatable to the taste of a gently bred young lady. Surely to God, you can't *really* be considering him as a husband. The man is a caricature. A regular Volpone in his raping of the nawabs."

Any fascination Samantha had felt for Lord Howard had diminished greatly during that luncheon. She thought silently for a moment, then changed the subject entirely.

"You wouldn't have heard from Ted or Bert yet, I fancy?"

"I only dispatched the letters this morning," he replied, and immediately returned to the more interesting theme. "I might rescind the order. I'm beginning to feel like one of Volpone's relatives myself, toadying up to Howard. A man can go too far in that direction. Money isn't everything."

"And besides," she said knowingly, "it is perfectly clear he plans to marry as soon as he can and set up a nursery of his own. I think you would be wise to treat him like any visiting relative."

"The problem is not precisely greed. Mama and I don't

85

want his gold for ourselves. It is merely our instinct, wanting to do the right thing for the boys.''

''Why can't they just marry heiresses, like all the other younger sons?'' she asked.

''We males of the Monteith line have the misfortune to marry where our hearts lead.''

Samantha knew that the late Lord Monteith had been considered unwise to marry Irene, who had no dowry worth the name. They came to a stile, and Monteith offered his hand to lead her over, but when they reached the top, he suggested they just sit on the fence instead. Before them lay the meadow, spangled with wildflowers waving lazily in the sun.

''I wonder how many *begahs* are in this meadow,'' he said idly. ''And how many *sicca rupees* it is worth.''

''Heed your own excellent advice, Monty. A foreign language is poor entertainment.''

''The primeval pastime of romance suggests itself, in this sylvan setting.''

''A pity you aren't accompanied by someone other than your sister. Mrs. Armstrong, for example.''

''That chaste lady?'' he asked, and laughed. ''She's already read my leaves, though rather unsatisfactorily.''

''Then I shall tell your fortune by plucking daisy petals,'' she decided, and hopped down from the stile.

Monteith didn't accompany her. He was content to watch her lithe young body bending and swaying as she garnered the blooms, with her skirt billowing occasionally when the wind caught it. He felt a hot anger building inside, to think of Howard pestering this young lady, who still seemed half a girl to him.

When she returned, Monteith took a daisy from her and said, ''Why don't I tell your future instead? I am not interested in attaching either a rich man, a poor man, a beggar man, or a thief.''

He pulled out the petals, one by one, and chanted the old saw, ending with the choice, ''Rich man.''

"The fates have decreed!" she said. "There is no arguing with a daisy. Howard it is."

"I mentally cast Howard in the role of Indian chief," he countered. "We have more than one rich man amongst us—Clifford, for example. And myself."

She felt him looking at her. A coil of excitement churned inside her, but her voice remained calm. "Then we must try another daisy," she said, and handed him one.

"Fate won't be managed in that way," he said, and tossed it aside.

She handed him another. "We teething infants are intractable. If you don't pull another daisy, I shall take my toys and go home. So there."

Monteith studied her pert smile and the clean line of her chin and neck as she tossed her shoulders playfully. When had Sam learned to flirt? Again the anger gripped him. "Are you practicing up your high spirits to tempt the Indian chief?" he asked in a thin voice.

"High spirits come naturally to a lady who is being courted."

Monty gazed across the field and suddenly jerked to attention.

"What is it?" she asked.

"It's a carriage. I wonder if Teddie—"

"No, it's Mrs. Armstrong's carriage!" Samantha said, and laughed. "Do you think Howard invited her to call?"

"Nothing would surprise me," he said, and leaped down from the stile. He held his arms up to catch Samantha. She put her hands on his shoulders and jumped off.

The sun cast gold lights on her blond curls. Excitement lent a flush to her cheeks, and amusement danced in her eyes. Between her partially open lips, he saw the flash of white teeth. Her small body felt warm and vulnerable under his hands. My God, she's beautiful! he thought, and held her a moment, looking up into her face.

As he swung her to the ground, he glanced a light,

sliding kiss off the side of her lips. "A brother's prerogative," he said.

Samantha stared icily. "It felt more like *droit du seigneur* to me!" she snipped, and turned aside.

"I must be slipping," he murmured, to cover his *gêne*.

It annoyed him inordinately that someone so sweet and innocent as Sam might be sacrificed to the vulgar taste of his uncle. Willingly sacrificed, which compounded the offense. Country girls should be simple. They should be able to accept a meaningless kiss, and not suggest there was some ulterior motive in it. Most of all, they shouldn't dangle after gentlemen old enough to be their fathers. He frowned and began walking at a brisk pace toward the Hall.

If the country was to provide no rest or pleasure, he might as well be in town. How had he allowed himself to get caught up in these country doings? Yet he was strangely interested in why Mrs. Armstrong had come to call.

Samantha was caught off guard by that kiss. Monty had never shown this brotherly regard for her before, and she knew perfectly well why he was showing it now. Despite his fine talk, he was just afraid she'd marry the nabob. As she hadn't shown any interest in Teddie or Bert, perhaps he'd been hinted to court her himself? Not to the extent that he might really be expected to offer for her—Monty was too much the gentleman to behave in such a scaly manner. No, he was just distracting her a little.

His long strides carried him a few yards in front of her, and rather than run to keep pace, she stayed behind. She admitted to a grudging admiration for his broad shoulders, the proud set of his head, and his manly vigor. Finally he stopped and waited for her. The carriage proceeded more quickly, but the shorter route lay through the meadow, and they reached the house just seconds after the carriage.

"Mrs. Armstrong isn't in it," Samantha said, peering into the carriage. "She's just sent her footman. What can it be? I wonder if he's bringing an invitation."

"No, a parcel," Monty pointed out, as the footman lifted a large square package wrapped in brown paper.

"The cat!" they exclaimed, and both hastened to the door.

The footman saw them, recognized Monteith, and handed the parcel to him. "Mrs. Armstrong says this is for Lord Howard, and here's a note to go with it," he said.

Monteith thanked him and took the package inside, where his mother flew into a pelter. "The sly wench," she snorted, when her son explained its arrival.

"She hinted she had given it to a charity bazaar in London," Samantha remembered.

"The cunning of her!" Lady Monteith scolded. "Let me see that note, Monty. I believe I shall hide it and say I found the cat in the attic."

Monty didn't reply, but he took the parcel to the hall and let out a "Holloa" in a creditable imitation of his uncle. It was used to summon not his own servants but one of the burra sahib's ghosts.

"For your master," Monteith said, and pointed to Lord Howard's hat, which had taken up semipermanent residence on the table in the front hall, much to Lady Monteith's chagrin.

His mother followed Monteith into the hall to complain. "Why don't you run upstairs and see what Howard has to say?" she suggested, by which he understood her completely: see if you can find out what is in the letter.

"I'm not that interested, Mama," he said, and returned to the parlor.

Lady Monteith was so consumed with curiosity and anxiety that she went upstairs herself, and was soon down with the whole story.

"I knew it!" she exclaimed, her fine hazel eyes snapping. "It was the cursed cat! She 'found' it in a closet, by means of emanations, if you please. I managed to get a glance at the note while he unwrapped it. These emanations, it seems, occur regularly when they are together. What the devil is she talking about?''

Mrs. Tucker nodded wisely. ''The only other customer who generates these emanations is Mr. Beazely, the rich old widower who owns the drapery shop and that row of apartments on High Street. *That* is the sort of emanations they are.''

''Surely Lord Howard doesn't believe in that occult foolishness!'' Mrs. Bright exclaimed.

''He'd believe anything a bold hussy like Armstrong tells him. And she signs herself Serena, if you please,'' Lady Monteith advised the company. ''I thought her name was Nancy.''

''I see you got a close glance at the note, Mama,'' Monty said with a satirical shake of his head.

The low cunning of Mrs. Armstrong's returning the cat and its probable consequences were discussed for several minutes.

''The likeliest outcome is that Lord Howard will call on her in person to thank her,'' Mrs. Bright suggested.

''Certainly he will,'' Lady Monteith agreed. ''That is the only reason she sent it, and he will know I gave the cat away. I shall say the servants did it in error.''

''The worst outcome,'' Monteith announced, ''is that he'll expect to put the horror in the saloon with the elephant's foot and the sword collection. I shall forbid it. I refuse to share the room with that monstrosity.''

Mrs. Tucker, who was fond of propriety, said, ''I believe cats were considered sacred in Egypt. I wonder if that is also an Indian belief.''

''Let him build a temple for it on the Langford property, then,'' Monteith said firmly. ''This is where I draw the line. The cat does not go into the saloon.''

''Think of your brothers, Monteith,'' his mother chided.

''Lacking in taste as they are, I cannot believe that either Ted or Bert will be offended at the lack of a stuffed cat in the saloon, Mama. They have survived without one all these years.''

There was no doing anything with Monty in this mood, and his mother let the matter drop. She had already set on a nice, dark, inconspicuous corner of the saloon for the feline, just to the left of the front window. It was as dark as the coal hole. Monty would never see it.

The guests were strongly inclined to remain till Lord Howard returned belowstairs, but a luncheon invitation was a luncheon invitation after all, and in due time they took their reluctant departure.

"Let us know what happens about the cat," Samantha said to Monteith before leaving.

"I have already told you what will happen. The cat remains in Howard's bedchamber. I am cured of the Indian fever. Of more interest will be to see what happens with yourself, Sam. I'll drop in this evening, if I may?''

"That won't be necessary. I'll monitor the curtain and time him in and out of Mrs. Armstrong's house. That was your reason for calling, was it not?''

He touched her chin with one finger. "No, the excuse. I fear he may slip across the street to visit you after. I shall be there to defend my sister.''

Samantha didn't return his playful smile. She just gazed from her deep, dark eyes. "Turning doctor, are you? You think to cure me of the fever by playing chaperon? Come if you like. You won't deter your uncle a jot—nor me, either. He'll do just as he wishes, as he always does. I wager I'll see the cat in the saloon next time I come.''

"What do you wager, Sam?''

"What it's worth to me. Tuppence." She laughed, and left.

Chapter 10

As feared, Lord Howard expected the stuffed cat that saved his life to be enshrined in the saloon, and as promised, Lord Monteith forbade it. Nor did he soften the blow by any excuse whatsoever.

"I hope you're not planning to put that thing in my saloon," he said curtly, when Lord Howard descended for dinner that evening. One of his white-clad servants walked behind him, carrying the glass case. "The room is already overcrowded with Indian gewgaws."

The nabob's brow puckered in quick anger. He gave Monteith a killing shot from his dark eyes, but after a moment, a smile broke. "It was my intention," he admitted, "but I can see the thing from your point of view, lad. These are *my* treasures; they'd mean nothing to you— why should they? They don't suit your more refined style." He spoke to the servant in some Indian dialect. The servant bowed a few times and disappeared back up the stairs.

Lord Howard turned an approving eye on Monteith and said, "It's high time you took hold of matters in your own house, lad. There's hope for you yet. I was beginning to fear you was tied to Irene's apron strings. It happens when a fully grown man still lives with his mama."

"My mother lives with me," Monteith said stiffly. "There is a difference."

"I daresay you'd get her blasted off if you was to take

a wife. I *do* like to see gentlemen married. It sets a good example to the countryside.''

"You may be sure I'll marry when I meet the lady who suits me.''

Lord Howard gave him a cunning look. "If someone else don't beat you to her," he said, and laughed as they went toward the dining room.

The speech conjured up the image of Samantha Bright. Monteith suppressed a sharp reply, but the warning rankled. Miss Bright was not the sort of young lady he intended to marry. She was rustic, not well dowered and not well connected. He could do a deal better for himself than a simple country miss. Yet he felt an intense aversion to her marrying this old yahoo.

After dinner, Lord Howard went upstairs and came down reeking of Steeke's lavender water. "I'd like to garner a bouquet from your conservatory, Monteith," he said. "You don't mind if I have my lads pluck a few blooms?"

"Lambrook is your home, Howard," Lady Monteith told him. "You must do just as you wish, mustn't he, Monty?''

"Help yourself to the flowers," Monteith said.

"Whom are you calling on, Howard dear?" Lady Monteith asked, her eyes kindling with apprehension.

"I am going to thank Mrs. Armstrong for returning the cat. And to discover how she comes to have it.''

Lady Monteith flushed. "Some dreadful misunderstanding—the servants—I asked them to make up a bundle for the church bazaar from the things in the attic. The idiots must have . . . You won't be long, I hope?''

"There is no saying. Don't fret over me, Irene. I ain't seven years old. I'm used to coming and going as I please.''

As Lord Howard drove into town, he decided it was time to remove to the inn. If he reached an understanding with Serena, he would want to be closer to her, and Irene's good nature was beginning to cloy.

He was greeted with warmth at the Armstrong residence. The palms were read again, and again strong emanations passed between the two. Serena was given to understand Lord Howard would be deeply insulted if she didn't accept a ruby ring as token of his gratitude for her returning the cat. She was also reminded of other baubles awaiting her pleasure, if only she could see her way clear to breaking a vow that was in no way binding. She stuck to her guns.

"I shall never remarry," she announced.

Lord Howard squirmed uncomfortably and, being an impatient man, came right to the point. "How about the other, then? A cozy little house in the countryside—"

"Ah, Howard," she said, with more sadness than rebuke. "If marriage is difficult, how impossible any other sort of alliance would be! I shall try to forget you suggested that." The "impossible" vow had been downgraded to "difficult," and she peered from under her long lashes to see if her caller had noticed it.

"The thing is, Serena," he said gently, "I have been bleating like a sheep at the Hall that I disapprove of widows' remarrying. I would look nohow if I turned around and married one."

She lifted her lashes and directed a long gaze on him. "It would take a very strong man to change his mind in public," she said.

"I haven't changed my mind."

"You are very foolish," she chided gently. "A woman is not a suit of clothing designed for one man only. She is a book to be read and interpreted. But I see you care a good deal for public opinion. I had not thought . . ." She came to a discreet stop, leaving her meaning for him to figure out himself.

"You're out in your reading if that is what you think! I do as I please."

"And it doesn't please you to marry me, I see." Her voice quavered, but she lifted her chin bravely. "We can still be friends, Howard. I hope you will call again, when you happen to be in the village. And now I must retire. I feel one of my headaches coming on.''

She rose gracefully. A long, loose robe fell in folds to her ankles, but clung enticingly to her upper body. The sleeves fell away to reveal a shapely white arm as she waved him good-bye. Lord Howard sat entranced at the picture.

He was not accustomed to having his character questioned. It riled him that this enchanting creature should think him so uncertain of himself that he dare not change his mind in public. Being very much a man of the world, he also knew she was angling for marriage, and that she was not of that class from whom he should choose a bride. She was not as easily available as he had first hoped, but like a nag with a bad knee, she just didn't go flat all around. He drew out his watch and checked the time. It was still early. He'd head across the street and flirt a little with Miss Bright. She was a fine-looking lady, and younger than Serena.

It added a fillip to the visit that Monteith was ensconced in the parlor, looking daggers at him.

''Congratulations, Howard,'' Samantha said. ''I hear Ginger has been returned.''

''That she has. I have just stopped off to thank Mrs. Armstrong for it.''

Lord Howard mentally compared the two ladies as he explained in detail the assault of banditti during which the cat had saved his life. Samantha had the unmistakable stamp of the lady. She was younger and equally pretty. Then, too, he had seen her in broad daylight, while Serena's charms had only been studied by lamplight. In spite of all Miss Bright's advantages, however, there was a certain something in Serena that whetted his more mature palate. She had the knack of appealing to a man's sensual nature.

Samantha made all the proper exclamations at his tale

of slashing the banditti apart with his *tulwar,* but in her heart she felt Howard would soon become a bore. The greater enjoyment of the evening was in annoying Monteith, who sat in well-simulated ennui.

"With my *creese* clamped in my teeth and my trusty *tulwar* in my hand, I had at them," Lord Howard said. "I caught one of them a good stroke on the wrist. I hope I didn't sever his hand, poor lout. Another crept up behind me and got hold of my nightshirt. I caught him by the shirttail and tossed him across the room."

Mrs. Bright clucked in disapproval, but Samantha smiled approvingly. "Then what? How many of them were there?"

"Only five, that I could see."

After fifteen minutes of Howard's boasting, Monteith rose and said, "I believe I'll be going home now. Mama is alone."

"That's right, lad. You run along and amuse your mama. I'll keep the ladies here lively."

Monteith glared at his uncle, who winked playfully at Samantha. Mrs. Bright looked up from her sewing and said, "It seems foolish, driving two carriages down from the Hall. Why did you not come together?"

"I don't keep a youngster's hours," Howard said.

"Then you should have called on Miss Bright first, Uncle," Monteith said. "She, I believe, does."

"I shan't overstay my welcome, never fear. I have a call to make at the inn before returning. I have decided to remove to the inn, Monty. I'll speak to the proprietor and see if he can clear the place out for me and my servants."

Monteith looked alarmed. "When did you take this decision?"

"Don't fret yourself. It has nothing to do with the decor of your saloon," he said playfully. "No, with my house to be built, I want to be closer to it. That's all."

Samantha wanted to hear about this decor of the saloon and accompanied Monteith to the front door.

"What happened? Have you come to cuffs with the nabob?" she asked eagerly. "Is that why you were in the sulks all evening?"

"Gentlemen don't sulk! I was merely peevish. And I have not argued with burra sahib. He agreed with me that a polite saloon was no place for his Indian artifacts. That's tuppence you owe me, miss."

"Put it on my account. My reticule is upstairs. What do you think of his moving to the inn?"

"I am delighted."

"Your mother won't be."

"I don't take orders from Mama!" he said with unwonted violence.

"I seem to have struck a nerve."

"Anyone's nerves would be exacerbated, living with that pirate. I don't know how you can fawn over him."

"I was not fawning!"

"Were you not? You never took that smile off your face from the moment he arrived. How a well-bred young lady can smirk and simper to hear of the wholesale carnage Uncle *allegedly* inflicts with one sword is beyond me."

"No, no! He had his trusty *creese* in his mouth as well. Imagine, there were five of them against him."

"There were three the last time he told it. Soon it will have been an entire regiment."

It was borne in on Monteith that he sounded like a jealous boy, and he smiled apologetically. "I'm being an unpleasant guest—and derelict in my duty besides. I promised I'd come to protect you from the nabob, and here am I shabbing off on you."

"He'll be leaving soon. And by the by, Monty, it wasn't necessary for you to make an issue of my relative youth. Howard knows my age."

"And you know his. If neither his advanced years nor his monologues, which we call 'conversation,' are enough to deter you, I fear I'm wasting my time in trying to protect you."

"True. You could be home playing whist with your mama," she taunted.

Monteith glared, but managed to keep his tongue between his teeth till he was beyond the door. On that unsatisfactory note Monteith left, and Samantha returned reluctantly to the saloon to hear more about *hoppos* and *hookahs* and *sircars*, till she began yawning into her fist.

At the Hall, Monteith was met by his mother, complaining that she couldn't call her house her own since Howard's arrival. "Here I have sat alone all evening. I daren't invite Clifford for fear of what Howard will think, and *he* walks off to the village to make up to that wretched Armstrong hussy."

"He didn't stay long. He was at Brights' when I left."

"All the worse! It is marriage with Samantha the old fool has in mind. From that Armstrong baggage to the daughter of a deceased half-pay officer. One hardly knows which is worse."

"You can hardly put them in the same category! Sam is at least respectable."

"I'm surprised Nora tolerates it. You should have stayed to keep an eye on him. And what were you doing at Brights'?" she demanded suspiciously.

"I'm not accountable to anyone for the visits I choose to pay."

"I hope you haven't been making overtures to Samantha. That's all I need, for that Armstrong creature to get her hands on Howard's fortune and you to offer for a nearly dowerless nobody. The boys will end up in the poorhouse."

"It's news to me if the Colonel Bright's daughter is a nobody!"

Their argument was interrupted by Cook, who came with her shoulders squared and her jaw set at a mutinous angle. "That Hindu in the kitchen has just destroyed tomorrow's bread," she announced. "He slid it into the oven before it had risen an inch. Either he goes or I go. I'll not have him sprinkling his foul powders in my food.''

"I'll speak to him, Cook," Lady Monteith said placatingly.

"Ho, *speak* to him. I've shouted at him till my face is blue, and he won't understand a word of English."

"I'll speak to Lord Howard. Can't you make more bread?"

"It's ten o'clock, and I can't get near the table for the bales littering the place. There's more of them landing in every day, full of heathen clothes and I don't know what all. Tomorrow his lordship's slaves plan to use the washing dolly, if you please. At least they've moved it out from the corner and begun taking out the water kettles. Tomorrow is supposed to be our laundry day. Though how we are to accomplish it with Jennie having to be sent home to escape the lecher, I don't know."

Lord Monteith sighed and tried to understand how his life had come apart. There hadn't been a moment's peace since the nabob's arrival. Serving maids were acting as footmen, and footmen were doing a sorry job of making beds. More parcels arrived from India each day, till you could hardly walk through the rooms.

"Lord Howard will be leaving very soon, Mrs. Jennings," he said.

"It won't be soon enough to suit me!" Cook snorted, and strutted off to her kitchen, muttering under her breath.

Lady Monteith emitted a yelp. "What do you mean— *leaving*?"

"He's going to the inn."

"What did you say to him? If you've lost his fortune, Monteith—"

"It was never ours to lose. He's leaving as soon as he can get space at the inn, and it won't be too soon to suit me."

"It's the cat. I'm having it placed in the saloon at once."

Monteith stiffened up like a poker. "No, you are not. And if you do it behind my back, I shall bust the glass and perform a feline suttee on the wretched thing, as we should have done when he sent it to us."

Lady Monteith wailed and ran upstairs to fling herself on her bed. Monteith drew a long sigh. Now he had alienated his mother, too. And there was still the cursed fête champêtre to be got through somehow. He felt a strong urge to flee. Brighton would be pleasant in June. Even London would be preferable to this pandemonium. But he knew he wouldn't go. He waited downstairs till his uncle returned a little later.

Monteith's face showed nothing but polite interest when he called for wine. Lord Howard looked at the servant and shook his head when she had left. "It must be Irene that hires your servants," he said. "Their chests are all as flat as pea on a platter. Not a full-bodied wench in the lot. What happened to the little redhead with the figure?"

Monteith poured two glasses of wine. "She's visiting her family till you leave. Pray leave your lechery at the front door when you enter my home."

"Servants expect a friendly pat here and there—it goes with the job."

"Not in this house. How did it go with Mrs. Armstrong?"

"I've come a cropper there, I fear. She is hinting at marriage, but I escaped unscathed. My old papa used to say if men could keep their lips and their trousers buttoned, the world would be saved a deal of bother. Truer words were never spoken. I'm happy to tell you I've kept both buttoned tight."

"It's an unlikely time to be looking for a mistress, when you're thinking of marriage. What are your intentions regarding Miss Bright?"

"I haven't quite settled on her, but she's in the lead. She is young, however. The youngsters don't make good lovers. That takes a little skill. I figure Mrs. Armstrong knows her way around a boudoir and back again. The way I see it, a wife has nothing to do with a mistress. A man likes dessert as well as meat and potatoes, what?''

Monteith's jaws worked in annoyance. "Which course of your feast does the wife represent, Howard?''

"Daily fare, meat and potatoes. I'd be discreet, as I promised. I was a little surprised to see you visiting the Brights again. You're sure I'm not cutting you out in that corner?''

"I am not paying court to Miss Bright.''

"Odd you end up in her saloon so regularly then. It might be best if you let off the visits for a while.''

"Afraid of the competition, Howard?''

"Devil a bit of it. I can hold my own.''

The two gentlemen exchanged a challenging look. Lord Howard set his glass on the table and said rather brusquely, "I'm for the goose feathers. Good night.''

"Don't let me detain you. Older folks require plenty of rest.''

Monteith took the bottle up to his room. Why was he behaving like a fool? Why was everyone else? Samantha imagining Howard was some romantic figure—a boiled cod had more romance in one fin than Howard had in his whole body. Meat and potatoes! Why was he himself going out of his way to antagonize the richest uncle in England? Why did he want to beat a man who should evoke nothing but laughter? The trouble was, Lord Howard had gone beyond a joke.

Chapter 11

Lord Howard drove into Lambrook immediately after breakfast the next day, explaining that he was going for another consultation with Gerard, the estate agent. "He is taking me through the house today. He was to approach a neighboring farmer about selling a few acres adjacent to the Langford property first," he explained. "I hope I will hear what the fellow is asking for it this afternoon."

This was an acceptable reason and gave Lady Monteith no fears of losing the fortune. Land was as safe as money in the bank. Her complaint was of a different nature when she sat with Monteith after Howard left.

"You should have offered to go with him, Monty."

"He would have asked me to accompany him if that was what he wanted."

"I wish he had told me last night he meant to be away this morning. I made sure he'd go into Lambrook this afternoon. I have asked Clifford to meet me at Mrs. Bright's at two."

"There's no reason you must be home every minute Howard is here. As to this foolishness of meeting Clifford at the Brights' house—"

"I don't want to do anything to upset Howard. Especially when he will be leaving so soon. I wish you could convince him to stay on here at the Hall."

"I wish I could convince him to leave today!"

"Think of your brothers, Monteith!" she said, with an accusing flash from her fine hazel eyes. "It is fine for you, with Lambrook Hall and the family fortune. What is to become of the boys?"

Monteith felt as guilty as his mother hoped. Primogeniture had favored him, but the boys were less comfortably endowed. "They're not penniless," he reminded her. "Teddie has Uncle Horace's estate—"

"A little farm in the wilds of Norfolk," she scoffed.

"Five hundred acres is only relatively small. Bert will be speaking to Lord North about a position at Whitehall when he finishes this holiday. He can live in the London house. It won't kill him to work for a living."

"It wouldn't kill you to show a little consideration to Howard, either! I swear you're going out of your way to disoblige me."

Monteith knew his mother would steal the cat's milk without blinking, but he *did* feel he should be a little more than polite to his uncle. In this indecisive mood, he shoved his cup away and left the room. He had matters to attend to around his own estate and spent the morning with his bailiff. When Lord Howard returned for luncheon, Lady Monteith was at pains to cement the bond between uncle and nephew.

"Did you arrange about buying the land, Howard?" she asked.

"Gerard spoke to the fellow this morning. I went to look at another place—the Grimsby farm."

"I hadn't heard it was for sale!" Monteith exclaimed in surprise.

"It isn't. I thought I might tempt him with a good offer, as the place isn't entailed, but he is quite adamant. It seems his family has been on that corner of land forever. Why that should stop him from turning a neat profit is beyond me. Sentiment has no place in business. If the man neighboring Langford will sell off a few *begahs*, I shall take the Langford place. Gerard will let me know this afternoon.

I'm taking another run down there to scout out a few features."

"Why don't you go with Howard, Monty?" Lady Monteith suggested. "You know all about land and crops and things."

Between guilt and curiosity, Monteith expressed agreement.

"I don't want to interrupt your usual schedule," Lord Howard said.

"I tended to my business this morning. I'll be happy to go with you, Uncle," Monteith repeated.

The flash that glinted in the nabob's eye didn't look like gratitude, but he said, "That's kind of you, Monteith. I plan to leave at two. And by the by, Irene, I am expecting some crates to arrive from London today. Will you be home? They are rather fragile—some antique statuary. I don't want the servants hauling them about and breaking them."

"I'll be very happy to take charge of them, Howard." She smiled wanly. There went the meeting with Clifford! And she couldn't send him a note, as he was taking lunch out with some business associates. Nora would be unhappy with the inconvenience, but she would at least send Nora a note.

"Are you riding or driving?" Monteith asked Lord Howard.

"Driving. Perhaps we should take your carriage."

"That's wise of you." Lady Monteith nodded. "The air is chilly by the seaside."

When the gentlemen left in Monteith's carriage, it came out that chilly breezes were not the reason for avoiding the open curricle.

"I am taking Miss Bright along to see the place," the nabob said.

Monteith felt a powerful jolt at the news, but to oblige his mother he said calmly, "As we have the carriage, perhaps Mrs. Bright would like to go along."

104

"She might as well. There will be no lovemaking with a third party present."

The third party realized this was a hint that he might find some other occupation. Instead, he began to speak enthusiastically about the excellent location his uncle had chosen and his eagerness to see it.

Lord Howard gave his nephew a suspicious look when Lady Monteith's footman was seen leaving the Brights' house. "What is this?" he demanded.

"Very likely a note from Mama," Monteith said. "She didn't know we were stopping, or I might have delivered it for her."

Mrs. Bright read that Irene would not be able to keep her assignation with Clifford, but as she had already asked the Russels to drop in, she had to refuse Lord Howard's invitation to join his party.

Samantha was happy to see Monteith had come along. Half her reason for accepting the invitation was to annoy him. His annoyance was taking on a coloring that spoke of more than mere peevishness. At times she almost suspected a tint of green. Why should he be jealous if he didn't care for her a little himself?

She wore her most flattering straw bonnet and put her hand on Howard's elbow as they left the house. From the corner of her eye, she noticed that Monty was frowning. No one noticed that Mrs. Armstrong was watching from behind her curtain. Her major occupation was scanning the street, especially since Lord Howard's return. She had seen his quick dart across the road last night. She had come to believe Miss Bright had attached Monteith, since he was at the house nearly every day. Howard's visit last night and that possessive hand on his arm aroused her anxiety. She immediately called her own carriage and threw on her bonnet to follow them.

Their route along the seacoast led her to believe it was only a pleasure jaunt. Unless they stopped somewhere for refreshment, there was no way she could join them. Her curiosity rose when the carriage turned in at the Langford estate. No one had lived there since she had come to Lambrook. In a twinkling, she figured that Lord Howard was thinking of buying the place. She didn't direct her driver to follow the carriage into the private road, but drove along half a mile and stopped. From this vantage point, she could see them when they came out.

Mr. Gerard was waiting for them at the house with the door open. "Everything is shipshape inside," he said. It was a happy day when Lord Howard had walked into his office and bellowed "Holloa! Is there anyone in?" Gerard's usually saturnine face hadn't been without a smile ever since.

"There is no hurry with that," Lord Howard told him. "Of more importance, did the neighbor agree to sell me that strip of land?"

"We were fortunate, sir." Mr. Gerard smiled. Good fortune dogged his every step recently. "It happens old Gilmore wants to retire—quit farming—but he doesn't want to leave the neighborhood. He will sell off his entire holdings, keeping only the house and a few acres for himself. He is willing to part with the whole thousand acres—for a price."

"I didn't expect him to give them away. Tell him I'm ready to close today," the nabob bellowed, without even asking the price.

"What is he asking?" Monteith inquired.

Mr. Gerard wrung his hands and said, "Ten thousand," in a quavering voice. Such sums were a new thing for him.

"That's pretty steep, Uncle," Monteith cautioned.

"Offer him seven-five," Howard said. "But I don't mean to lose out on the sale for a piddling twenty-five hundred pounds. See if he goes for the lower figure, and if he don't, raise it by five hundred till he says yes."

"I fancy eight thousand will take it," Gerard said.

"Since you don't plan to farm, why don't you only buy

106

half the acres?'' Samantha suggested. "It seems a shame to put so much land out of production.''

"I don't like to be cramped,'' Howard told her. "There will be the gardens, you see. That will eat up a couple of hundred. And that entire strip,'' he said, pointing down the hill to the bay, "will be taken up with my docks and boats. You are forgetting the tide, my dear. I shall have to put in a little canal and a lock to control the water level. It don't do a ship any good to be beached. Hard on the hull. I would prefer to keep it wet at all times. And there will be the buildings for overhauling the vessels.''

"But there is all the land that goes with the Langford estate itself,'' she pointed out.

"My horses must pasture somewhere. I mean to set up a stable and training track for them. We Monteiths have always been interested in racing. You don't want the stench too close to the house proper. Then there will be my hunters and hounds to put somewhere. The stable hands will need somewhere to rest their heads as well. Perhaps in the little house already standing,'' he said, glancing to the Langford mansion.

"Oh, Howard!'' she gasped, shocked at such an extravagant way of going on.

He grabbed her fingers and squeezed them. "I forgot. That is to be your little playhouse. The stable hands must be closer to the horses in any case. Then I'll build this squat little hill up a few hundred yards and put our house here, facing the sea. My statuary will go behind it. I am having a little Indian temple shipped home as well, in pieces, to be reassembled. Some dandy carving on it. A little naughty you will think when you see it, but we'll keep it out of bounds of the kiddies.''

Samantha noticed the bent of his talk—as though it had been decided she was to live here with him, and he hadn't even asked yet. Monteith noticed it, too. He gave her a look, half questioning, half quizzing. But when he spoke, it was of other things. "What size of house do you plan to build?" he asked.

"Nothing elaborate. I'm a simple man. Say—forty or fifty bedchambers, but perhaps a little larger area on the ground floor. There will be the picture gallery and the library and half a dozen or so saloons. A ballroom, of course—nothing fancy. What I won't skimp on is my conservatory. I want to be able to walk through groves of palmyra and coconut trees as I did in India. Unfortunately, they'd perish in the cold here, so I must enclose them. Well, what do you think of my plans, missie?"

"I think it is the entire island of England you will need, Howard," Samantha said in a weak voice.

He slapped his knee and laughed merrily. "I don't aim so high, but if the Isle of Wight were for sale, I'd pick it up. I hear it has an excellent climate."

"Shall we have a look at the inside of the house?" she suggested.

"That is of little interest to me," he said with a kindly smile. "You go ahead. I want to pace out the location for the temple. I had planned to root out that little orchard," he said, waving toward a thriving fruit orchard of two hundred trees, "but I begin to think my temple would look well with it for a backdrop. I like the effect of old stone against new greenery. It reminds me of home—Lambrook Hall, I mean. A pity there isn't a lake on the property. In the future, I might snap up the property on the other side and have one dredged out—stock it with fish."

Mr. Gerard mentally rubbed his hands in glee. "I'll keep an eye on that property for you, Lord Howard." He smiled, and went trotting off after his patron.

Samantha, with her head spinning, went into the Langford house. It was roughly five times the size of her own home, and five times as elegant. A crystal chandelier graced the front hall. Marble floors stretched like a black-and-white-checkered sea before her. In the distance, an elegant horseshoe stairway curved upwards. She looked back toward the open doorway, where Monteith stood watching her. She sensed his indecision, and to encourage him to join her, she spoke.

"Can he possibly be serious about all these plans?" she asked. Her voice echoed in the empty hall. "It begins to sound almost like madness."

With this slim encouragement, Monteith stepped in. "He's serious. When the madman is a millionaire, we call it eccentricity. Do you dislike his ideas?"

She shook her head in bewilderment, and they began strolling around the downstairs. "It's like asking me if I'd like to be the queen. It sounds too farfetched to be taken seriously."

"You must have noticed the courting is stepping up in pace. Last night he told me you were number one. It seems he's decided—one of these days he'll remember to pop the question. You must do battle with your conscience and decide what you'll say."

"It will take years to do all the work he speaks of," she parried. "There's no hurry."

"I sense a note of reluctance to come to grips with the issue."

"It's not reluctance. It's incredulity. To think, just a few days ago I was bored!"

"That's not surprising. Just last night I was bored to flinders at your house."

She gave him a pert look. "Thank you, Monteith. Naturally we simple country folk can't expect to amuse a London rattle when he decides to make a sojourn."

"I was bored with his infernal ranting about *tulwars* and banditti, not with you."

"It is unlike you to be so gauche," she said, hoping to lure him into more personal conversation.

He ignored this taunt. "The long evenings of Indian tales go with the territory, remember!"

"Is this why you invited yourself along on the excursion, to warn me?"

"Uncle didn't say you were coming with him till after we had left the house."

Samantha was disappointed to hear it. "What a lovely saloon," she said, looking around at the embossed ceiling and matching fireplaces of white marble.

"It seems a shame to desecrate it with weapons and other Indian paraphernalia."

"You forget, if I am the chosen one, this is to be my own personal playhouse. I can do as I please with it. I shall spend a good deal of time here, and I shan't allow a *tulwar* or scimitar anywhere near it."

"What pleases you is to avoid any reminder of your husband, I see."

"I didn't say that!"

Monteith raised a finger and shook it playfully. "You did, you know. There was also an intimation that you'd get away from him as much as possible. A strange way for an infatuated fiancée to speak."

"I am not infatuated, and I'm not a fiancée either."

"It would be kind to disillusion him now, if you don't plan to accept."

She regarded him suspiciously. "You're in a great hurry for me to turn him off. He'll only go haring off after someone equally ineligible, you know."

"I can't undertake to guard the entire female population of Kent. It is only *you* I have sworn to protect."

"It's the family fortune you're protecting, not me."

She cast a bold, questioning stare at Monteith and was confused by what she saw. It wasn't love shining in his eyes, yet not dislike, either. It was frustration. Monteith didn't know his own feelings, but he knew that, for whatever reason, he wasn't going to let Sam marry his lecherous old uncle, not if he had to offer for her himself.

"The two are not mutually exclusive," he parried. "I am protecting you from the insidious lure of fabulous wealth, and the money from you."

"Not necessarily in that order."

110

"In either order. My old nanny used to say money married is hard earned."

"No doubt that's where the famous Monteith tradition of marrying for love came from."

"No, it's older than that. My papa, you know, followed it, and he had a different nanny from me. Tradition isn't built in one generation."

They left the saloon and went into the library, where empty shelves reached to the ceiling. From the French doors they looked out on a cobbled garden, bordered with yews. "How lovely!" Samantha exclaimed. "A secret garden! Let's go out, Monty. They've left the stone benches and table."

They went out into the sunlight. An arch through the yew hedge led them to a parapet overlooking the sea. "I love this house just as it is," Samantha said softly. Why couldn't she be here with some other suitor than Lord Howard? "It would be a crime to turn it into some pseudo-Indian temple. I wonder what sort of architecture Howard has in mind."

"Ask him," Monteith said. "He's coming back now."

Samantha was aware of a stab of disappointment. She looked over her shoulder and saw Lord Howard eagerly climbing the hill toward her, with Mr. Gerard puffing up after him. As she looked, the two men turned aside and stopped. She and Monteith exchanged a questioning look and began descending the hill to see what had caught Howard's interest.

They saw Mrs. Armstrong's carriage pulling up the drive. She had become tired of waiting and taken the matter into her own capable hands. Anyone might stop to have a look at a property that was posted for sale. Who was to deny that she was interested in buying it herself?

Samantha and Monteith joined Howard and Gerard, and they all went forward to greet Mrs. Armstrong, who smiled in well-rehearsed surprise.

"Good afternoon," she said. "Don't tell me I have

competition. I made sure no one else was interested in this property. It has stood vacant for months. I decided to have a look around and see if it would suit me.''

Lord Howard sprinted forward and held the carriage door for her. "I'm afraid I've beat you to it, Serena. I have as well as signed on the dotted line. I didn't know you had any intention of moving.''

"One feels cooped up in town. I like to see open ground around me and the sea beyond.'' As she spoke, she looked all around with a deep sigh. "Odd that we both felt drawn to this spot, Howard,'' she said in a soft aside.

They joined the others, and though Mrs. Armstrong had no real interest in buying the house, she wanted to see it inside. "May I have a little peep around?'' she asked Mr. Gerard.

"There can be no harm in it,'' he agreed. "Why don't we all go?''

Lord Howard wasn't eager to make the trip with his two flirts, and said, "Sam has already looked around. Monteith will entertain her.''

Monteith lifted a satirical eyebrow at Sam. She smiled demurely and said, "I should love to see the playhouse again, Howard. I'll go with you.'' She turned to Mrs. Armstrong and said, "Lord Howard planned to raze the house, but I convinced him to save it. He is going to raise this squat little hill a few thousand feet and build a castle on top.''

Monteith didn't plan to miss this tour, and joined himself to the party, to walk again through the downstairs rooms. Mrs. Armstrong appeared quite calm in the face of all Lord Howard's grandiose schemes, and even added to them.

"Of course you will want a gazebo, Howard. Perhaps atop a second little mountain at the side of the main house. Something in the nature of the Prince of Wales's Brighton Pavilion—but in miniature, of course. Your guests will enjoy to see your fleet of ships setting out to sea. I envisage crimson and purple sails.''

"And saffron!" Samantha threw in, "for your own catamaran, Howard.''

"I am not into such lively colors myself, but if it would please the ladies, why not?''

"Of course you will have a knot garden," Mrs. Armstrong urged.

"And your own herb garden to grow curry and Indian spices," Samantha added.

"The spices will do better in my conservatory, I fancy," Lord Howard suggested.

"Ah, yes, along with the palmyras and coconuts," Samatha said.

In the clear light of day, the nabob soon discerned the trace of the crow's foot around Serena's eyes. This lessflowing robe betrayed a certain breadth of figure that went beyond the desired fulsomeness, too. Mutton dressed as lamb was the phrase in his mind. Her constant squeezing of his arm, though pleasant, was recognized as unladylike. As the tour progressed, it was to Samantha that he turned the greater part of his attention. He noticed the warming up of her interest and was inclined to settle the matter as soon as possible.

Serena saw which way the wind was blowing and decided to try the efficacy of jealousy in bringing Howard to heel. She turned to Monteith and said, "Shall you and I step outside and stroll through the orchard? It is a shame to waste such a day indoors.''

He was too polite to refuse, but she realized Lord Monteith was not happy to leave. His mood had the tinge of jealousy, but perhaps he was only miffed to see his uncle setting up a flirtation with Miss Bright. Naturally he would prefer to see Howard and his fortune remain single.

Howard watched them leave and turned a playful eye on his partner. "We are rid of them at last," he said, and patted her fingers. "It is only natural Serena should prefer

113

a noble young buck like Monteith, I expect. But that is nothing to me. I am not about to set up a light-o'-love when I have marriage on my mind, eh, Sammie?''

Her smile faded and she looked listlessly around at the library. "Perhaps we should be returning to town," she said.

"It is Mrs. Armstrong's arrival that has put you out of sorts, but I didn't arrange the meeting. She is not the sort of female you ought to be with. She snatched up a ruby ring as quick as winking this morning, and that, you know, shows pretty well what she is."

"It also betrays a streak in yourself that I cannot approve, Lord Howard."

"Now you are piqued with me, and I had hoped we might have an intimate coze—about marriage, lass. What do you say I speak to your mama and set myself up as a regular suitor? I am not one to shilly-shally around when I have made up my mind."

"No, really—"

He regarded her closely. "Don't be shy to say what you think. I am not a lady, to be sinking into a decline at a refusal. I must know the truth. At my age, I haven't a moment to waste. I realize some ladies prefer those niffy-naffy lads like Monteith. He'll not show you a better time under the covers than I, if *that* is what worries you. My hair may be gray, but my passion is red-hot, I promise you."

Samantha blinked and turned bright pink. "Really, Lord Howard!"

Again he studied her. "Then there *is* something between yourself and Monteith? I don't mean to tell tales out of school, but on the other hand, I ought to mention—he told me flat out he was not courting you."

Anger was added to her sense of outrage, and she strode swiftly from the room, to meet Lord Monteith and Mrs. Armstrong coming in. Monteith took one look at her pink

114

face, her flashing eyes, and clenched jaw and went pacing forward.

Lord Howard came, laughing, to join them. "I've trod on the young lady's sensitivities," he said, and laughed. "But what I said about my gray hair is true, all the same," he said waggishly to Samantha.

"What is true?" Monteith demanded stiffly.

"You don't want to know, Monteith," Samantha replied tartly. "Comparisons are odious. May we leave now?"

Conversation was noticeably stilted as the horses drew them back to Lambrook.

"I'll just let you down and walk you to the door. I cannot go in, as I want to go to the inn and put a rocket under them about clearing out the place for me," Lord Howard said.

"I can find the door by myself, thank you," Samantha said. With a curt nod, she hopped out and ran to the front door.

Chapter 12

Reverend Russel and his wife were just rising to leave when Samantha entered the Willows. She made a few polite comments to her mother's guests before going upstairs to put off her bonnet and pelisse. She was in such a temper she wanted to be alone for a while. Monteith had been right all along—she was not dashing enough for the nabob. For Howard to speak openly to her about the muslin company and his own red-hot passion—really, the man had no more notion of propriety than a heathen. Her flesh crawled to remember the lascivious light in his eyes during that brief talk. Obviously she couldn't go on pretending to be flattered at the attentions of such a creature.

She came up short on the unspoken word "pretending." Was that all it had been? Were her gay smiles at the Langford house only to show Monteith she could outdo Mrs. Armstrong? She couldn't care less if Lord Howard had a dozen mistresses. What rankled was the bald assertion that Monteith had no interest in her. He had actually told Howard so.

Downstairs, Mrs. Bright frowned at Mr. Sutton and said, "I wonder what that wretched nabob did to put Samantha in such a snit. I can't for the life of me imagine what she sees in the old pelter. If Howard were younger and refined—like yourself, Clifford—I'm sure I could understand it. Of course, she is very pretty—there is no mystery in what he sees in Samantha.''

Mr. Sutton stroked his chin and smiled. ''We know who Lord Howard had in his eye first, Nora, till he learned you were a widow. I remember the first words he uttered after saying good evening to us at the Hall. He turned to you and asked if you were married.''

Mrs. Bright blushed. ''I'm sure that was not his meaning. No gentleman has looked at me in a decade.''

''You're wrong there, my dear. Many a gentleman casts covetous glances in your direction.'' His softly beaming eyes suggested that he himself was not entirely innocent. She felt a fluttering in her breast and a strange buzzing in her ears. Such sensations hadn't afflicted her since her courting days with the colonel.

She had always found Clifford extremely attractive. As he was Irene's beau, however, she had never allowed these feelings to take root. Nor had Clifford shown any more than a friendly interest. What had caused him to speak now? He was miffed at the way Irene was treating him, of course.

''I never pretended to match Irene for looks,'' she said. ''She is a very attractive lady.''

''She is, but since Lord Howard's coming—well, one ought not to speak ill of the absent, but I cannot like the underhanded way she is managing things. Foisting me off on you,'' he said. ''I shan't pester you again, Nora. It was ill done of me to go along with it.''

''I'm sure we all go along with what Irene says. And I enjoy your visits, Clifford. Truly, it is no imposition.''

''Kind of you to say so. I enjoy them, too.''

''Irene might go into one of her huffs if you object.''

''Let her!'' he said. ''A man has to make his own decisions. I either go to her at the Hall or I don't see her at all. Truth to tell,'' he added daringly, ''I shan't mind so much if she gives me my congé.''

Nora felt a warmth rise up in her body and began speaking vigorously about the weather. Clifford had mentioned leaving with the Russels, but he passed his cup and settled in for more tea and conversation.

The Brights were dining with the Russels that evening, and when the reverend hinted he could use some help in mending the hymn books, they both volunteered. Neither one wanted to be at home to receive a call from a gentleman, nor did either particularly wish to make the other her confidante. Mrs. Bright sternly told herself Clifford hadn't meant a thing by his little compliments. He was always such a good-natured, obliging gentleman—it would be foolish to make too much of it. Enjoying the luxury of having an intrigue all to herself, she failed to notice her daughter's mood.

When Lord Howard came thumping on the door at ten-thirty the next morning, Samantha ran upstairs to her bedroom, claiming a sick headache. The nabob came in with his usual gruff good cheer.

"I'm sorry to hear Sammie has the megrim, but it gives me a chance to speak to you alone, Mrs. Bright. I fancy you have a pretty good idea why I'm here?"

"Well—"

"You're right. She's the little lass for me. I have come like a proper young suitor to ask permission to court her. Thank you kindly," he rattled on, before the poor lady had time to draw breath. "I knew you would be all for it, but I mean to dot all the i's and cross the t's. You have only to name your dowry."

"I'm afraid Samantha has only five thou—"

"Ho, ho, ho," he bellowed, slapping his knee. "That was not my meaning, dear lady—Mama," he added roguishly. "I wouldn't dream of robbing you of any part of your pittance. What price are you asking for her is what I meant. Don't be bashful. I'm willing to go as high as fifty thousand."

"Fifty thou—"

"All right then, sixty. I don't haggle when I want something."

"Indeed, that was not my meaning!" Mrs. Bright gasped. "How very generous. I—I shall tell Samantha," she said.

"I gave the little lady a hint of my intentions the other afternoon. It won't come as a complete shock to her. Her taking such an interest in Shalimar encouraged me to suspect I would not be rejected."

"Shalimar, you say? I didn't hear Samantha mention—"

"That is what I'll call the place. It is a famous garden in Kashmir. I mean to duplicate something of the sort at my place. We'll be happy to throw up a little dower house for yourself as well, missie, if you care to join us. I daresay Sam would have no objection to your living in her dollhouse. She plans to keep the Langford place for her own amusement," he explained when Mrs. Bright frowned at this peculiar offer.

"The Langford house—yes, I see," she said, bewildered. Why had Sam not mentioned any of this?

The call was interrupted by the arrival of Clifford Sutton, bearing a bouquet of flowers from his conservatory.

Flushed with success, the nabob greeted him with a crippling swat on the back. "Another suitor, eh?" He laughed. "It must be the balmy spring weather. I shall leave and let you two get on with it. But don't you forget my offer, missie. You would be very happy at Shalimar. I'll come back later to plot out the *burrakhara* and *nautch*. We will want a proper feast and celebration to honor the occasion. Perhaps the dancing girls might go amiss," he added, his brow pleated with a frown. He stroked his chin and left.

"What did he mean by that?" Clifford asked suspiciously. "Why is he pestering you with talk of feasts and celebrations?"

"He has offered for Sam. Sixty thousand pounds, Clifford!"

"Good God!" Mr. Sutton exclaimed, and turned pale. His flowers hung by his side, forgotten. "I was afraid it was yourself he had come for."

Mrs. Bright felt again that warm rush of blood, the buzzing in her ears. A watery smile flooded her face. Upon seeing it, Clifford assumed much the same expression, as he handed her the bouquet.

"Thank you," she said, and immediately tried to turn the visit to its proper course. Unfortunately, her voice betrayed her by rising to a squeak. "Irene didn't tell me she would be meeting you here this morning, Clifford."

"She won't be coming, Nora."

Their eyes met in guilty pleasure. Mrs. Bright called Foley to arrange her flowers and led her guest to the morning parlor. "Can you stay for a cup of tea? Perhaps Irene will drop in . . ."

"I wrote and told her my decision," Clifford announced manfully. "My footman brought a note back. It says—and I quote her verbatim—'If you cannot behave like a *gentleman*, Mr. Sutton, I cannot continue seeing you.' "

"She never called you Mr. Sutton!"

"That may be *my* fault. I addressed her as Lady Monteith." He pulled out the much-read note and handed it to Nora. " 'Not behave like a gentleman,' mind you!" he said, fuming with rancor. "Accusing me of shabby behavior, after what she has put me—*us*—through! Honorable gentlemen don't go slipping behind the backs of brothers-in-law, who have nothing to say about anything. I mean to answer that note and tell her exactly what I think. I consider myself entirely at liberty," he added, to make his point crystal-clear.

But still he was uncomfortable courting before he and Irene were formally through, so the conversation turned to Samantha's offer. "Why did he say you would be welcome at that foreign-sounding place?" Clifford asked.

"That was what made me fear—er, think—he had offered for yourself."

She related any item of interest she could remember regarding Shalimar. What stood out in her mind was the sixty thousand, but what rested at the bottom of her heart was a reluctance to see Samantha marry such a tiger.

"I cannot like to discourage her—such a grand match!— but, oh, dear, he is so loud and foreign-looking," she worried.

"She will certainly never get an offer to equal it, from the worldly point of view."

"Oh, no, indeed! Monteith himself hasn't half so much money. If I thought she really cared for Lord Howard, I wouldn't have a word to say against it."

Clifford assumed the male's prerogative of telling her what she should do. "Tell Samantha his offer," he advised. "Neither encourage nor discourage her. Sam is a sensible girl. She will make up her own mind, and we shall support her in whatever she decides."

The telltale "we" came out so naturally Clifford didn't even notice it. What was in his mind was that Nora would be all alone once Samantha married. He knew the nabob's way of rushing at things as if there were no tomorrow. The wedding might very well take place within a month. What better and more natural time for Nora to settle elsewhere?

His own courting would be difficult, as any local outings would also involve Lady Monteith. There was the fête champêtre that was fast expanding into an orgy, with a ball to follow at Lambrook Hall. Naturally, Nora would want to attend that, and so would he.

After Clifford left, Mrs. Bright went upstairs to tell her daughter of Lord Howard's offer. Mrs. Bright had no intention of pressing her daughter, but she couldn't keep the enthusiasm from her voice when she echoed the wonderful words, "Sixty thousand pounds! So generous! And he offered to build me a dower house as well—or to let me live in the Langfords' house.''

"But money aside, Mama, what do you think of him? His character is far from steady, you must know.''

"You are thinking of his son, who died in India.''

"That, and his chasing after Mrs. Armstrong.''

"I daresay all the English bachelors in India carried on with the local women. About Mrs. Armstrong—I cannot feel he would expect to do anything like that after he married a young bride. Marriage might be the very thing to stabilize him. But it is up to you, Sam. You're old enough to know your own mind. I have nothing to say against it. What you must ask yourself if whether you would be happy living in a castle and married to a millionaire. Always bearing in mind, of course, that the millionaire is the nabob,'' she added scrupulously.

"Aye, that's the rub,'' Samantha said, and drew a long sigh.

"He's very good-natured and would give you whatever you wanted—*more* than you wanted, for your tastes are simple like my own. If only he weren't so loud and—raucous.''

"And old,'' Samantha added. "It isn't a decision to take in a minute. I'll think about it.''

After Mrs. Bright left, Samantha lay on her bed thinking. Her mother's bright eye and air of excitement suggested she favored the match. Her whole conversation had been encouraging. It was a life that sounded like a dream—except for Lord Howard. If only it could be Monteith . . .

Monteith, of course, was definitely not interested in her, and was at pains to announce it to his uncle. It would put Monty's aristocratic nose out of joint if she married Howard. As appealing as this was, the price to be paid was very high. She was extremely loath to accept the nabob's offer, yet common sense and ambition lured her toward it. She must see more of Howard, see if it was possible to tame his Indian ways. And if it gave Monteith a few bad days while she made up her mind, that was unfortunate but unavoidable. Her lips curved in a parody of a smile as she considered the next few days.

Lord Howard returned that same afternoon to take Mrs. Bright to see the site where Shalimar would be built. Of course Samantha accompanied them. The ladies heard tales of the beautiful Vale of Kashmir, which was apparently Howard's goal in landscaping Shalimar.

He took them to the top of the "squat hill" and gazed across the water. "This reminds me of Kashmir," he said softly. "You come from the wretched, hot misbegotten plains of India up past Tibet and Nepal, and it's like entering paradise to feel the gentle breezes. There high up in the mountains there is a green oasis of lakes and lotus blossoms and rivers. We hired a *shikara* and sat under the canopy while our rower took us down the Dal River. You could see the mountains reflected in the water as clear as a picture. What a sight! And it's even better at night, with moonbeams dappling the water. I wish I could take you there, missie."

He wiped a tear from his eye as he remembered that trip with Jemdanee. "But I shan't tackle India again. I was thinking in terms of France and Italy and the rest of the continent for a honeymoon, while the builders put up Shalimar for us."

Samantha's mind drifted off to the boulevards of Paris and the fountains of Rome. She had always wanted to travel. If she didn't marry Howard, the alternative was not some other eligible match but spinsterhood in Lambrook. Howard seemed less loud today. In this more subdued mood, she almost felt she could find some happiness with him.

Then he turned away from the water and gazed up to where the mountain would rise. "I have been thinking of having Shalimar faced with marble," he said, "with a few domes and minarets in the Indian style. The Taj Mahal is a dandy building. Folks would see it from the sea as they sailed by, and say 'An eccentric nabob built that for his lovely young wife.' That was how the Taj Mahal came to be built, you know.''

Samantha glanced at her suitor and felt some stirring akin to love at this romantic notion. She would be remembered throughout history. She wished Howard would hold her fingers and squeeze them, to show he was thinking in the same vein.

Howard shook his head and said, ''The Taj Mahal was the lady's burial tomb. I have heard it cost four hundred lakhs of rupees.''

How very appropriate. Shalimar might prove her tomb as well.

''What is a lakh, Howard?'' Mrs. Bright asked.

He was easily diverted to talk of money. ''A hundred thousand. It was almost impossible to calculate such a sum. And people think *I* am rich. I am a pauper next to Shah Jahan.''

They took a quick look through the house. Samantha noticed her mother's interest. How Mama would love to live here, in Langford's gracious home. It would be good to have her close by for company. And as Mama grew older, she wouldn't have to worry about her being alone. There was so much to recommend the marriage Howard offered! But she had told him she wanted a week to consider it, and she would take her seven days.

They drove home to the Willows. Lord Howard didn't accept an offer to stay for tea. ''I have to hire a builder to get busy on planning Shalimar. I shall run to London and hire the fellow who builds palaces for the Prince of Wales. I daresay he would do well enough. I shan't be here to press my suit for a few days, missie,'' he added.

''You'll miss the fête champêtre,'' Mrs. Bright exclaimed.

''We'll have another when I get back. Now I would like to say farewell to Sammie.'' A commanding look was directed at Mrs. Bright.

She took the hint and left the lovers alone. "Since you want to keep me on tenterhooks for a week, I might as well get the house started," Howard said. "There is no point wasting time. The sooner it is built, the sooner we can move in and start filling up the nursery."

To hear the seven days of courting described as a waste of time did nothing to soften Samantha's feelings. There was surely a hint in his speech that her breeding potential was a strong feature of the marriage as well. Naturally, she wanted children, but "filling the nursery" of such an enormous house was an appalling prospect. And how was she to get to know Howard better when he was in London? His assuming that he had already been accepted was another annoyance.

"Do you really feel this is the proper time to go?" she asked. Frustration lent a sharp edge to her voice.

Howard nodded his head and winked. "Absence makes the heart grow fonder, so folks say. If I come back any fonder of you than I am, we had best post the banns before I go." He tried to pull her into his arms.

Samantha pulled back. "I haven't accepted your offer, Howard!"

"Heh, heh. You are a clever little minx. Whetting my appetite! You need not fear such tricks are necessary. I am very eager to have you."

Without further ado, he lunged at Samantha and crushed her against his chest. His strong arms closed around her, and his lips began chasing hers as she squirmed and wriggled to be free. There was no escaping him. He soon caught her head in the palm of his hand and attacked her in a fierce kiss. One hand began groping toward the opening of her bodice. She pushed him back and tore out of the room without so much as a good-bye.

Lord Howard left the house frowning. A shy young filly. He would have to dull his appetite while in London or she'd bolt on him. Indeed, dulling his appetite was half the reason for the trip, as Mrs. Armstrong was proving such an evasive mistress.

Sam sat in her room, trembling. Her anger at Howard's leaving had turned to relief. When he returned, she'd tell him she had decided they did not suit. His only disappointment would be in the few wasted days. Let him buy some other lady to fill up his nurseries. She'd rather remain a spinster than be subject to his pawing.

An hour later, a great, gaudy diamond-and-ruby engagement ring arrived at the Willows by messenger. Samantha put it in the bottom of her drawer so she wouldn't have to look at it.

Chapter 13

The days after the nabob's departure provided a much-needed period of calm in the emotional turbulence of Lambrook. Lady Monteith, brooding upon recent events, came to think of Howard as a tropical storm that had blown through the neighborhood leaving chaos in its wake. It seemed she hadn't a friend left to her name. She had come to cuffs with Monty and most of her staff; she and Clifford were no longer on terms of civility—who would have thought Clifford capable of such a rebellious streak? She had heard distressing rumors of visits to the Willows by Clifford, even after he refused to meet her there. Was it possible Nora was trying her hand at stealing Mr. Sutton? If so, it meant she had lost her best friend. She could hardly continue on terms with Nora if Clifford offered for her.

The fête champêtre, which had been expanded at much cost in money and labor to an all-day-and-half-the-night celebration for Howard's amusement, was scheduled to occur during his absence. And to top it all off, Howard had offered for that provincial miss, Samantha Bright. Such a prime piece of news as that wasn't long making the rounds. No one told Clifford it was a secret; naturally, he had told his sisters and mentioned it to the Russels. By the time church let out on Sunday, the whole neighborhood was aware of the event. Samantha felt like Mr. Dod's three-legged chicken when she walked up the aisle, with every head turning to stare at her in rampant curiosity.

The stares from the Monteith pew bristled with hostility. Monty cast a glare that would wither fruit on the vine. His mama didn't trust herself to do more than give one sharp, rebukeful look that encompassed both mother and daughter in its condemnation. How anyone was expected to think holy thoughts in such a seething cauldron of ill will was beyond Samantha. She looked at the pretty stained glass windows and found her mind wandering to the heathen temple the nabob planned to set up on his estate. It had "naughty statues," he had said. A rueful smile tugged at her lips. She heartily wished he had left the building in India, and himself along with it. But soon it would all be over. She'd reject Howard's offer, and things would return to normal.

Just how far they had been diverted from the norm was borne in on her after the service, when Monteith bowed coolly and took his mother's arm to lead her to their carriage. Lady Monteith didn't even nod. The fact that Clifford Sutton was fast legging it toward them had something to do with that, of course.

St. Michael's was only a short distance from the Willows, and in fine weather the Bright ladies didn't have their horses put to. Mr. Sutton offered them a drive home, but they declined, to deflect any further hostility from the Monteiths. Whether Irene was any less furious to see Clifford walking them home than driving them was a moot point. By the time they reached the door, the Monteith carriage was well beyond view, and Clifford was invited in.

"I was never so uncomfortable in my life," Mrs. Bright said when they sat at the table with a cold luncheon before them. "Really it is the outside of enough that Irene should cut me dead in front of all my friends. And she cut you, too, Clifford. I hope you didn't say something rude to her."

128

"Say?" he asked, lifting his eyebrows up to his hair-line. "You must know I am no longer allowed to *say* anything to Irene. The rupture occurred by post. She had the gall to write and say I might call on her, as Lord Howard would be away for a week—after I told her I wouldn't be led by her brother-in-law."

"Did you answer her note?" Samantha asked eagerly. Her mother's romance was of nearly equal interest with her own.

"Certainly I did. I told her that as Lord Howard no doubt planned to return, I saw no point in resuming a friendship that would so soon be interrupted. She sent back a few baubles I gave, and all my letters," he announced happily. "That means we are through." A soft smile beamed on Nora, who smiled through her frowns.

"I cannot see our way clear to attending the fête champêtre when the host and hostess ignore us," Samantha announced, and looked hopefully to her elders for guidance. She didn't want to miss the fête. It was working up to the major social event of the season, and probably the last one that Howard wouldn't attend.

"I wouldn't dream of going," Clifford replied. "I shall have a fête of my own on the same day—just for us," he said.

Three people hardly made a fête, and Mrs. Bright said, "Perhaps your sisters would come to yours."

"They've already bought tickets and new bonnets for Irene's. If they don't attend, we won't have firsthand news on the Monteith gala," Clifford pointed out.

"Not have firsthand news, with the Russels and all the town attending?" Nora asked. "We shall know everything that happened, every word spoken, and every bite eaten. But I do dislike being at odds with Irene. It is so uncomfortable. We have been bosom bows for decades."

"All that will be patched up when Sam marries the nabob," Clifford assured her.

Samantha stirred restively in her chair. Her mother, under Clifford's guidance, had come out in strong support of the match. Not only was it a grand connection, but it would smooth her own path to marry Mr. Sutton. Samantha hadn't told her mother about Howard's attack in the saloon. She was too embarrassed and too shy. Attack was really the only word to describe his leap on her. Perhaps it was how married people behaved, but if that were the case, the parties involved would have to be very much in love to tolerate it. She knew she must tell her mother that she had decided against the match, however, and this seemed the proper opening for it.

"Actually, I have decided not to marry Lord Howard," Samantha announced calmly. The only symptoms of her discomfort were two scarlet patches splashed on her cheeks.

"Not marry him!" Clifford exclaimed. "My girl, you're mad. He's rich as Croesus."

"I assure you that sacrifice is not necessary, dear," her mother said. "You must not let Irene's sulks deter you from such an excellent parti. All will be forgiven once you are mistress of Shalimar."

"My decision has nothing to do with Lady Monteith," Samantha said firmly.

"But why are you refusing him, then?" Clifford asked. "You're the envy of every lady in the parish—in all of London, I daresay. Why, Howard's the catch of the decade."

"He is extremely eligible, Sam," her mother added.

"But I don't love him, you see. Nor do I particularly want to be as rich as Croesus. I'm convinced I should be quite uncomfortable in a marble palace, surrounded by foreign servants I cannot even talk to."

"You'd soon catch on to the lingo," Clifford assured her.

"The honeymoon in Paris, Sam!" her mother reminded her. "I thought you were looking forward to it."

It was clear they didn't understand. They were going to

ask a million questions and pester her. "Not with Howard!" Samantha said, and fled from the table, holding her napkin to her lips.

"Well!" Clifford said, and looked to his hostess for enlightenment.

"I wonder what's gotten into her?" Mrs. Bright mused.

"Last-minute jitters, perhaps?"

"It seemed like more than that. When Sam speaks in that prissy way, she is usually hiding something. I wonder if there is someone else. . . ."

"Teddie was always fond of her," Clifford mentioned. "Irene used to say that if his Uncle Hiram left him a few thousand, they might make a match of it."

"Sam never mentions Teddie or Bert from head to toe of the week. Dear me, I wonder if it's Monteith she has in her eye. He has been calling more often this spring than ever before."

Clifford looked worried. "Irene won't countenance that. She cannot bear-lead Howard, but she keeps a firm grip on her boys."

They discussed Samantha's inexplicable behavior till lunch was over, then moved out to the garden to enjoy the sun and flowers. From her bedroom window, Samantha looked down on them. They looked contented, like a happily married couple. Clifford was a kind, good man. He'd make an excellent husband for Mama, and she'd make him a better wife than the demanding Irene. She knew her rejecting Howard was a rub in their path, but she couldn't face life with Howard. She'd rather marry the dustman.

At Lambrook Hall, the Monteiths were also distressed. "I expected better of the Brights," Irene scolded, stabbing angrily at a plump shrimp. "Not content with stealing Howard's fortune, they must have Clifford's as well. It's so unfair, Monty!"

Monteith felt like a caged lion. Roaring and gnashing his teeth ill became a grown man, however, so he attempted to be ironic instead. "If you will remember,

Mama, I told you it was pointless trying to lead Howard. If Sam refused him—''

A snort of incredulity greeted this. ''Much chance! She trapped him into it, the sly miss, pretending butter wouldn't melt in her mouth, and all the while she was making up to him behind our backs.''

Monteith's jaws worked, and he continued, ''If Sam refused him, he'd only marry someone even less eligible.''

''He'd have to go back to India to find someone less eligible than that rustic.''

''She will make me a charming aunt.''

''Yes, when she grows up! And that doesn't excuse Nora for stealing Clifford!''

''Well, Mama, you treated him like an old shoe. What do you expect? I have more respect for Sutton than I ever thought I would have.''

''And I've lost Nora, too,'' she moaned, and finally shoved away the plate. The cold shrimp sat like a chip of ice in her throat, refusing to go down. ''They'll never come to the fête champêtre now. We've expanded the thing to last a whole day and night. I cannot face it, Monty. I shall take to my bed and claim a sick headache.''

Monteith also pushed his plate away. A black scowl rode on his brow, and his voice sounded dreadfully like his papa's. ''No, Mama. You will don your best bib and tucker and show the town what you're made of. We Monteiths don't buckle under that easily.''

''I wonder if Clifford would come if you asked him, Monty?'' she suggested, a ray of hope lighting her eye. ''I doubt he'd have the gumption to say no to you.''

''And you actually love such a gutless creature?''

''Monteith! Watch your language!'' She folded her napkin in her lap and said uncertainly, ''It's not that I love him, precisely, but he is good company. He always lets me win at cards and is willing to take me anywhere. It is lonesome, Monteith. You forget I am here alone nine-tenths of the year. And I dislike the Dower House. It is

132

so dreadfully dark, with that yew hedge shadowing the windows. And the rooms so small. Naturally, I shan't go on living at the Hall after you bring home a wife."

"That isn't about to happen in the near future."

"You never know when the arrow may strike," she warned.

The footmen began placing dishes on the table. The very smell of hot meat was like an emetic to Monteith. He actually felt ill. *You never know when the arrow may strike.* It had struck some time within the past week; he had acknowledged it even more recently. When Howard came home boasting of having "snatched the prettiest little lady in Kent" was when the shaft entered his heart.

Monteith had begun feeling ill at that moment. Ill and angry and desolate. "She hasn't accepted!" he had exclaimed, before he got a rein on his temper.

"You may consider the bargain settled," Howard had said, smiling. Monteith had willed down the urge to strike that gloating old face. "And a hard bargain they drove, too, but I consider her worth every penny."

A satirical gleam from his nephew's eyes was all that was required to elicit the exact sum. She had sold herself for sixty thousand pounds. That was the sum and the total of it. Sam, with her innocent freckles and her quaint manners, was just another fortune hunter when all was said and done.

He was furious with himself as well as her. He had been too slow, had had too high an opinion of himself. In his pride he couldn't believe he had fallen in love with Sammie Bright, who had loved him forever—well, liked him anyway—and would certainly have snatched at an offer. His having fallen victim to her provincial charms should have been a boon to her. He should be playing the role of knight on a white charger, carrying her out of anonymity to a life of wealth and privilege. What did the wretched girl do but find herself a knight who could carry her higher and faster. He couldn't compete with white marble palaces and a million pounds.

"When is the event to take place?" he had asked Lord Howard, through stiff lips.

"As soon as I get back from London. I am taking your advice and going there this very day to arrange for the architect. But don't fret, I mean to saddle you with my bride. We'll tour Europe on our honeymoon while the castle is abuilding. Sammie wants to see Paris."

Monteith was stirred from these unpleasant memories by his mother's voice. "I'll write the note, and you deliver it," she said, looking at him with a curious eye.

"I beg your pardon? I was woolgathering."

"The note—to Clifford. I wonder if he's left the Brights' yet. I know perfectly well Nora would urge him to stay for lunch."

Monteith's aversion to asking Clifford to attend the fête champêtre began to fade. "I could hardly deliver such a note while he's at the Brights' without asking them as well," he pointed out.

Irene gave a *tsk* of annoyance. "We might as well face facts. Sam has got him; there's no point cutting off our nose to spite our face. I have no wish to be excluded from the doings at Shalimar. The whole world will be down to visit them. Urge Nora and Sam to come to the fête as well. It will only fuel the rumor factory if they aren't here."

Lord Monteith spent fifteen minutes in the arrangement of his cravat and put on his best jacket before going to pay the call. He felt as nervous as a bride when he lifted the brass acorn knocker at the front door of the Willows.

"Good afternoon, milord." The butler smiled. "The mistress is entertaining in the garden. I'll take you out."

"Is Miss Bright there as well?" Monteith asked.

"Miss Bright is upstairs, sir. Was it the young lady you wished to see?"

"No! That is—yes, if you please." He hadn't foreseen the possibility of being alone with Sam, but it was not an opportunity to be missed when it occurred so naturally. "I'd like a word with her as well, if she is not indisposed."

Samantha heard the bell and hopped up from her bed to hang over the banister, from which vantage point she could hear without seeing or being seen. The voice she heard set her heart pounding eagerly. Her curiosity and hope soared together to great heights as she scampered back to her chamber to make hasty repairs to her toilette.

When she descended the stairs a moment later, her hair had been brushed till it shone, and a smattering of powder subdued the sprinkle of freckles across the bridge of her nose. Now that she had the opportunity to meet Monteith face-to-face and alone, her former pessimism was blended with a pleasant, tingling excitement. She assumed he had come to hint her out of accepting Howard's offer, and meant to pay off a few old scores. It was a change for her to have the advantage of him, for once! She'd make him squirm before telling him her decision. How angry he'd be that he had lowered himself to come, once he learned it wasn't necessary.

As soon as Monteith saw the glitter of mischief in her eye and the pert smile on her lips, he stiffened to a ramrod. His lips thinned and he spoke harshly.

"I see you're chirping merry at your conquest, Sam."

She eyed him with amusement. "What conquest is that, Monty? Oh—I daresay you're referring to Howard's offer. And I didn't even have to learn to read the leaves." She sat on the sofa and nonchalantly arranged her skirts around her. "To what am I indebted for the honor of this call?" she asked with a bland smile.

Monteith looked at the sofa a moment, and took up the chair facing it, as he didn't want to betray any eagerness to be close to her. "Mama wished me to ascertain that you and your mother still planned to attend the fête champêtre tomorrow."

Sam gave him a long, searching look. "I believe not,

135

if the chilly stares received from your pew at church this morning are an indication of how we shall be received.''

He jerked his shoulders in a movement at odds with his usual composure. ''Mama was in a bit of a pucker about this Clifford thing, but—''

''What accounts for *your* glares, Monteith? I made sure you would approve of any disturbance in that quarter. It wouldn't be Howard's offering for me that accounts for your frowns?''

''No!'' he said quickly, angrily. ''Although I will say I'm disgusted to hear of the settlement you demanded.''

She allowed a cool tinkle of amusement to issue from her throat. ''Demanded? You misconstrue the matter! I'd be bathing in diamonds if Howard had his way. So generous,'' she added, to goad him.

''You might have screwed him up to a hundred thousand if you hadn't been so eager to have him!''

She swallowed her anger and answered with forced civility, ''The eagerness was all on Howard's side, I promise you. I haven't quite agreed to have him, actually.'' She peered to see if Monteith showed any interest in this leading speech.

His brow darkened and his jaws worked. ''You're even more grasping than I believed. You didn't need *me* to hint that a higher dot might be managed by a little well-timed reluctance, did you?''

The unfairness of this charge was a goad to her proud spirit. Worse was Monty's complete lack of interest in her reluctance to accept Howard. ''After all, he *is* worth a million, as he is so fond of announcing. A lakh is only ten percent of a million, you must know. A lakh is a hundred thousand, Monteith. I mention it as you seem to have missed out on the trick of speaking Indian when trying to bring Howard around your thumb.''

''Unlike your cunning self!'' he charged, and jumped to his feet to pace the saloon. ''You work fast, Sam. I have to give you credit for that. I thought if I could get him blasted off to London before—'' He came up short on this betraying speech.

She stared while a well of hot anger steamed up in her breast. She rose to her feet to confront him. ''*You* urged him to go! He even *told* me so, and I never suspected why! You thought he'd forget me if you sent him away. And you accuse *me* of cunning!''

Monteith wheeled around and faced her. His livid color only accentuated the white line around his lips. His nostrils flared as he prepared his setdown. ''I tell you to your face, madam, you are a cunning, conniving, vain, self-seeking, provincial fortune hunter. You set your cap at Howard to show me you could get him—to flatter your vanity and teach me a lesson.''

Samantha gasped at this outrageous charge. For a full fifteen seconds she was speechless. When she recovered her wits and tongue, she lashed out at him. ''I never fully appreciated the vastness of your arrogance till this minute. You actually think my accepting him involved *you*, in some manner. I assure you, a relative stranger who shows his face in the county two or three days a year does not feature that prominently in my life.''

''Are you trying to make me believe you love him? You love that swaggering, bilious, bragging, rough-tongued old lecher?''

''I never said I loved him.''

Monteith's face stiffened like a starched collar. ''Then you admit you're just after the money!''

''Certainly not!''

''Are you not?'' He grabbed her two arms and held them in a painful grip while his dark eyes blazed into hers. ''Tell me you're not. Tell me you love him, if you can say it without blushing, and I'll know you're a practiced liar. You're marrying him for his fortune.''

This loaded command was met with a flash of violence. Samantha wrenched her arms free and turned on him like a Fury. Her breath came in quick pants. ''I'll tell you nothing, sir. Who I marry is none of your business. And why I marry him is my own affair. What does your concern amount to but a will to keep Howard's fortune for yourself? You don't give a Birmingham farthing whether I'm in love, or happy, or *he's* happy, as long as the million is safe. You don't even care whether your own mother is happy! You think you're the center of the universe, that the whole world revolves around you. Your nose is out of joint because a better man has come along to call the tune. You're no longer the lord and master, ruling everyone. Well, I take pleasure in telling you, Lord Monteith, you don't rule me.''

''When have I ever tried to rule you?''

''You're trying now. Why did you come here but to argue me out of accepting Howard's offer?''

''Do you love him?'' he asked, and stood firm, pinning her with his eye.

Beneath the frustration and anger that glittered there, Sam thought she discerned a glimmer of something else. If it was love . . . She tossed her head and looked away, waiting for him to say, or do, something. From the corner of her eye, she saw his rigid form and heard only the echo of his quick, shallow breaths. The silence stretched till she wanted to scream. When she could endure it no longer, she said, ''Love isn't born in a minute. It may take time, but no doubt it will come. Howard is a very passionate lover.''

His movement was so quick she didn't have time to move. His arms flashed out and grabbed her fingers in his, crushing them till they ached. ''Are you telling me you let that lecherous old lout get his hands on you?''

She looked at his fingers gripping hers, then looked at Monteith with a meaningful light in his eyes. ''The Monteiths, in my experience, have never waited for permission before placing their hands on a woman. Howard is rough, and woos not like a babe. But then Howard may be forgiven—*his* intentions are honorable.''

Monteith heard that meaningful accent and through the cloud of anger tried to interpret it. He was on the edge of declaring his own honorable intentions. His fingers worked nervously on Samantha's, clutching and slowly inching up toward her wrists as he braced himself for his declaration. She sensed what was in his mind, and waited.

When the silence stretched uncomfortably, Samantha spoke again to bring the issue to a head. "Naturally, I shall accept him," she said firmly.

Jostled out of his hesitation, Monteith heard himself say in the stern accents of a judge, "You will not. I *forbid* it!"

It was not the speech she expected to hear. The moment of possible reconciliation was over. Samantha swallowed her disappointment and tried for an air of ironic levity. "Do you indeed, milord? Go ahead—forbid it till you're blue in the face, but I will marry Howard, with or without your sanction or permission. If you wish to make an egregious ass of yourself by trying to stop us—"

Monteith dropped his hands. Unthinkingly, he ran one through his hair, disturbing its careful arrangement. "Sam, this match is not right for you!"

"No, Monteith; it's not right for *you*! You've done your duty by warning me of the dangers of a good and lawful marriage. Your conscience may rest clear that you've done all in your power to save the family fortune. I assume that this invitation to the fête tomorrow was to cement family ties. I'm sure Howard would dislike to be at odds with his kin, so Mama and I shall attend."

She made a graceful curtsy and said before parting, "Pray deliver my compliments to Lady Monteith, and tell her I look forward to seeing her tomorrow. She will be anxious to see my engagement ring." On this parting shot, she swept from the room.

Monteith stood on a moment alone, wondering where he had gone wrong. At length, he went into the hall and got his hat. He remembered, before leaving, to pass Mr.

Sutton's invitation to the fête along to the butler, as he couldn't face more company.

Samantha went to the front window to watch him leave. One lone tear oozed out of her eye and slid unnoticed down her cheek.

Chapter 14

Monteith met his mother as he went storming into Lambrook Hall. "They're coming to the fête," he said.

Lady Monteith regarded his glowering visage and knew that conversation was pointless. "That's fine," she said wearily, and their conversation was at an end.

At the Willows, Samantha reported Monteith's invitation at more length, but her emotions were equally upset. She felt reduced to a pulp. Before long, she realized what a dreadful ordeal the fête would be. On top of everything else, she had told her mother she wasn't marrying Lord Howard, and she had told Monteith that she was. Lord Howard's proposal would certainly be the chief item of conversation between the two parties. She must change her story to either her mother or Monteith. Backing down in front of Monty was unthinkable. She wouldn't do it. Yet did she want to spite him enough actually to marry Lord Howard and live a prisoner at Shalimar?

After Clifford Sutton's departure, she began to smooth the thorny path before her. "About Howard's offer, Mama," she said hesitantly, "perhaps I was a little hasty. I don't mean that I shall have him, necessarily," she added quickly, when her mother broke into a hopeful smile. "It is only that—well, Monteith was so arrogant, there was no bearing it. He practically demanded that I not accept, so I let him believe I would marry his uncle."

"Oh, Sam," her mother said, and shook her head in reluctant sympathy. "You can't go on like this. You must settle the matter one way or the other. What was the nature of Monty's concern?" she asked, and gave her daughter a thorough scrutiny.

"Fear of seeing Howard's fortune go out of the family, of course. What else would it be?" she asked with a shrug of brassy indifference.

"I have wondered—he seems to come here very often recently. I thought perhaps there was something between you two."

"Oh, there is, Mama. There is a great deal of animosity. He despises me nearly as much as I despise him," Sam replied.

But despising didn't bring a choking sob to a girl's throat and tears welling up in her eyes. Mrs. Bright watched ruefully as Sam darted upstairs. So that was it—the poor child had developed a tendre for Monty. How very complicated life became when men entered the picture. And how interesting!

The day of the fête dawned warm and bright. From her bed, Sam looked at the cloudless sky with loathing. She had hoped for a torrential downpour to postpone the great day. Intricate plans had been laid regarding the Brights' attendance. Their visit was to be more than a courtesy call, less than full involvement. They would arrive in midafternoon to watch the races and take tea, but not remain for the alfresco dinner. For the first half of the affair, Clifford would not accompany them, though he would be there. There was no reason to rub Irene's nose in her defeat. Clifford would, however, escort the ladies to the Hall for the first half of the ball that evening. By that time, Irene would be accustomed to Mrs. Bright's victory, and not create a scene. At the intermission, all three would leave. The only maneuver not settled was whether they would leave before or after the late supper.

Lambrook was a hive of activity in the morning as everyone darted to the shops, picking up a last-minute piece of ribbon or pair of hosiery. To get in the early part of the day, Samantha and her mother joined the throng on High Street. After lunch, they went upstairs to make their toilettes. Samantha's finger was nearly worn out putting the great, ugly engagement ring on and off. She had no wish or real intention of marrying Howard. No announcement had been made. To appear in public wearing the ring would definitely confirm the engagement, and this idea was repulsive. Yet she had boasted to Monteith that she would wear it.

When she left the house, the ring sat in her reticule. It was much too large to fit under her gloves. By midafternoon, Monteith and his mother were on thorns wondering whether the Brights would come.

"Where are they?" at one o'clock had changed to "They're pretty late," by two. By three, Lady Monteith had wandered off to the shade of an awning for some peace and quiet, to distance herself from the high-pitched squeals of the smock races. When her son joined her, she said, "They're not coming. Are you sure they said they would?"

"Yes."

"Clifford, too?"

"He'll come if the Brights come."

"I wish he would come without them. I wager Nora has him cornered in her saloon this minute. They're in league together to snub us."

"It's just as well," Monteith said, and looked through the throng again for the only one of the party that interested him. When he realized—or imagined—that his mother was suffering, too, he remembered Samantha's accusation of selfishness and regarded her with a sympathetic eye.

"Do you really mind very much about Clifford, Mama?"

143

"I mind the shame of losing him to her."

"Yes, but has losing him inflicted a heart-wound?"

"Heart-wound?" she asked, staring. "Where do you pick up such sentimental rubbish? Heart-wound, indeed! I have been amidst gentlemen long enough not to have any heart. I was hoping for a good set-to with the pair of them. If I can't have a husband, I shall at least have the pleasure of a juicy scandal. I intend to be extremely rude to the senile young couple. A few playful sallies about limping down the aisle—perhaps a hint that Sam's fiancé is a decade older than her mother's—well, half a decade."

Monteith looked at her in wonder. Here he had been pitying her! His own intention was to behave impeccably toward Samantha, to make up for his former boorishness in her saloon. Blighted love had dulled his claws, it seemed, while spiteful pique had sharpened his mother's. It was himself he should be pitying.

Yet when he finally spotted Sam's straw bonnet coming in at the gate, he felt such a jolt of anger stab him that he knew he would not be so suave as he had intended.

"Here they come!" he said, and took his mother's elbow to lead her forth.

"No, Monty. Not yet. We shan't go running after them. Let them come to us. Is Clifford holding her elbow?"

"Clifford isn't with them."

"Good!"

The tardy duo were in no hurry to seek out their host and hostess. The Brights stopped and were stopped to exchange a few words with so many friends that at last Monteith could endure it no longer and went forth alone.

He thought Sam had never looked more beautiful. This was the proper setting for her, a country party, with the sun casting dappled shadows on her face through the loose weave of her bonnet. It glinted on her curls and shone full on her gown, whose provincial cut went unnoticed. Monteith's gaze didn't get below her chin. Her eyes glittered like star sapphires, and her lips, half open in nervousness, spoke to him of ripe cherries.

"Welcome to the fête!" He smiled, and had to force his attention to the older lady to include her. "Mama has sought refuge under the awning. I'm sure she'd like to see you, Mrs. Bright."

"We'll step along and say good day," Mrs. Bright decided.

Monteith placed himself between the ladies with a hand on each one's elbow to hurry them toward the awning.

Lady Monteith lifted her snapping hazel eyes and said, "Well, Nora, you came alone, I see. I expected you would be with your new beau."

"I came with Samantha. Clifford should be along shortly. A lovely party, Irene."

"And Sam," Lady Monteith continued, shooting sparks at the daughter. "You, too, are bereft of your fiancé. It must seem quite like old times, both of you without a man."

"You, on the other hand, always have dear Monteith to keep you company," Mrs. Bright retaliated.

"A blessing, I'm sure." Sam smiled demurely.

"Get us some wine, Monty," his mother ordered. "Not that wretched orgeat, mind. Do sit down, Nora. At our advanced age, we can't be standing in this heat."

"No, indeed!" Mrs. Bright agreed, with seeming timidity. She sat and added, "I must reserve some energy for the ball this evening. Clifford has asked me to save him the first dance."

Foreseeing a verbal fencing match, Samantha agreed to go with Monteith to fetch the wine. "Let them go to it," he said, leading her away.

"Your mother started it!" Sam said quickly.

At the refreshment booth, Monteith asked a footman to take a bottle of wine to the ladies. "Sam, what will you have?"

"Wretched orgeat will do for me."

He got two glasses and looked around for a private bench. "Don't let me keep you from your duties, Monteith," she said primly.

"The party's been under way for hours. My duty is done for the present. And I want an opportunity to apologize for yesterday's outbreak of poor manners. You were quite right to chastise me."

She waited, hoping to hear why his temper had reached such a pitch. At length she replied, "No permanent harm done. A storm will often clear the air."

"You arrived very late. We began to wonder if you were coming at all."

"An entire day of sun and noise and squealing children is a little more than I enjoy." With a sudden urge to enliven the conversation, she added, "I find I prefer the calm of older companions now."

Her goad had the desired effect. Monteith's precarious calm was shattered. "You refer to the calm bellowing of your fiancé, I assume? Do you prefer it with or without the theatrics of *creese* and *tulwar*?"

"Ah, you are learning the language! Too late, Monteith. The damage is already done."

"No, only instigated. You haven't got him to the altar yet, milady."

"Well begun is half done," she taunted.

"Damage is an odd way to speak of your coming marriage."

"I was considering it from your point of view. Unlike some, I don't always think of myself."

"I personally never stood to gain anything from the nabob, if that is what you're referring to."

"Not precisely to gain, but it would prevent a loss. You wouldn't have to provide for the boys if Howard did it for you, I suppose."

"I found having him around the house was too high a price to pay. I hope you don't make the same discovery, when it is too late."

"Kind of you to be concerned for me. Shalimar will be big enough to lower the din by distance. If the clashing of swords becomes too tiresome, I can always retire to my toy mansion on the lower hill."

Monteith set his glass aside and frowned into the distance. "I had hoped we wouldn't come to cuffs today, Sam. I've had my say about you and Howard. I know I said it badly, but the intention was good, whatever you may think."

It was a peace offering, and as an afternoon and evening of squabbling was too long to endure, Samantha let the argument fall to the ground. "I understand. It must have come as a shock, his offering for me so soon. I'm sure Howard will do something for the boys, Monty. He's very generous."

His head slewed around, and his anger was fierce. "I hope you don't think that is my main concern!"

She looked a sharp question at him from her brightly glittering eyes. It almost seemed he might say the magic words to cut through the Gordian knot. With all her willpower, Samantha silently prayed that he would. Unfortunately, Mrs. Armstrong chose that inauspicious moment to intrude. Unsure of the polite hour for arrival, she had waited till she saw the Brights' carriage leave before calling her own out. She came, apparently already dressed for the evening ball, in a green silk gown and bright gemstones.

"What a grand frolic, Lord Monteith." She simpered.

He rose and offered her a seat. "What's that you're drinking?" Mrs. Armstrong asked, before he had time to offer her a drink.

"Orgeat, but perhaps you'd prefer wine," Samantha said.

Any suggestion that Mrs. Armstrong would not prefer the beverage of ladies was snorted aside. "What you're having will suit me."

Monteith went to fetch her orgeat, and Mrs. Armstrong

turned to Miss Bright. ''I hear you got an offer from old Lord Howard. Congratulations, Miss Bright. Can I see the ring?''

''I—I'm not wearing it,'' Samantha said. It sat like a bomb in her reticule, but she didn't want to bring it out for Mrs. Armstrong's exclamations and, no doubt, comparison with her own. That Mrs. Armstrong knew Howard's offer was about as good as saying the whole town knew.

Mrs. Armstrong rubbed her ruby carbuncle against her silk skirt and figured she had got all she was going to get out of Lord Howard. ''Lud, what a ruckus,'' she said, looking toward the races. ''I have half a mind to slip home and come back for dinner. I wonder why Monteith entertains such a parcel of riffraff.''

''It's a charity affair; the public is invited.''

''If this is John Q. Public, they can keep it. Ah, there is Mr. Beazely!'' she exclaimed, and leaped up from the seat just as Monteith was returning with her orgeat. Hanging on to Beazely's arm, she sallied forth, her peregrinations much enlivened by such a rich and single companion.

Monteith shrugged and drank the orgeat himself. It was difficult to get the conversation back on the track after this interruption. Discussion dwindled to isolated remarks about the party, and soon Samantha left. She was tired of the din and wandered around to the private gardens, where the unruly children weren't encouraged to go, though a few adults strolled through the rows of rosebushes.

She sought out an isolated corner by the Italian fountain and sat with her chin on her hands, thinking. It was very odd, the way Monty had flared up at her for saying Howard would do something for the boys. *I hope you don't think that is my main concern!* But if not that—the money—then what? What else did the marriage involve, except herself? That was what bedeviled her as she sat alone, thinking. Twice now it had seemed Monty was on the verge of declaring himself. Was it her imagined status as an engaged lady that deterred him? Had she outwitted herself by letting him think she had accepted Howard's offer?

As she sat inhaling the sweet aromas of the garden and looking at the roses and the silver shower of water tinkling in the fountain, a ripe rose fell apart before her very eyes. A shower of fleshy pink petals drifted slowly to the ground. Three wafted into the fountain, where they swirled in lazy circles. She took the fanciful notion it was Monteith, Howard, and herself adrift there. As she watched, the petals were pulled along toward the drain. They spun in dizzying circles a moment, before disappearing down the black hole—all three of them.

It wasn't just her own life she was on the verge of ruining. What kind of a wife would she make Howard, disliking him as she did? And if Monty *did* love her . . . Three lives ruined, all for lack of someone speaking up and saying what was on her or his mind. It was insupportable for a colonel's daughter to be so cowardly. But did Monteith love her? That was the overwhelming question.

Chapter 15

A prickly truce was established between the Monteiths and Brights. Mr. Sutton, perforce, was included in the uneasy peace. Mrs. Bright expressed the general feeling when she said after the afternoon fête, "I felt as though I were treading on eggs, but at least we didn't break any."

Mr. Sutton, still stinging from a few verbal wounds, modified it to, "Walking on broken glass was more like it."

"Has it been decided whether we shall remain for supper after the intermission tonight?" Samantha asked. No further opportunity to sound Lord Monteith out on his feelings had occurred during the afternoon.

"That depends on whether we're enjoying ourselves," her mother said.

"And whether Irene is serving lobster patties and champagne," Mr. Sutton added.

Such elegant treats would not be served at the barn dance for the whole town, but only for the elite at the ball.

As Samantha made her grand toilette for the evening, she realized that this might be her last opportunity to see Monty before Lord Howard returned. She had an instinctive feeling that once the nabob was back in town, the situation would become even more difficult. That gentleman had a knack of stirring up trouble.

As the party from the willows planned to leave the dance

early, they found it did not diminish their dignity to arrive on time. Mrs. Bright wondered if Clifford felt a pang when Irene opened the minuet without him. In former times, this honor had often fallen to him. Lacking an escort who could incite jealousy in her erstwhile lover's bosom, Irene chose her son. This was a lapse from strict protocol, but at country dos the niceties were often bent. On this evening, for instance, the butler wasn't announcing arrivals.

The party from the Willows slipped in unnoticed and joined a large table of friends, including the Sutton ladies and their husbands. Mrs. Tucker was decidedly displeased with Clifford's new attachment, and showed her displeasure by staring with sad eyes and sighing at Irene as she performed the maneuvers of the minuet with her son. Samantha, on the other hand, was now a lady to be courted, and Mrs. Tucker offered her husband to Sam for the next set. After Mr. Tucker, Clifford had a round with Sam. Then it was the country dances that required a younger partner to withstand the strenuous exertion.

Clifford's other sister, Mrs. Jenkins, put her husband forward to accompany Samantha for the cotillion. The dinner hour was drawing near, and still Monteith had done no more than stop by their table a moment, chatting to them all. As no champagne was being served, Sam feared they would leave before dinner. Though the dance thus far had been a tedious affair, she was eager to stay. It was Lady Monteith who unwittingly arranged it.

After the cotillion, Monteith got his mother aside and said, "You're making a cake of yourself, Mama, pretending the Brights and Suttons aren't here. For God's sake, go and talk to them."

She made a resigned grimace. "I intend to, Monty. Fiddlesticks, what do I care for losing a beau? I can always find another. Where shall I find two such good friends as Nora and Clifford? I'll ask them to join us for dinner."

And so it was arranged. They all sat hodgepodge at an informal round table. When Monteith rushed to draw

Sam's chair, she thought he would sit beside her, and her heart swelled in hope. Alas, Mrs. Tucker nipped into the next seat and pointed her husband toward Samantha's other side. She had heard such marvels about Shalimar that she was eager to ingratiate herself with the future Lady Howard. Monteith took up the chair beside Mrs. Tucker, and spent the dinner hour looking at the back of the lady's head, for Mrs. Tucker forgot to converse with anyone but her quarry. Samantha was forced for an hour to discuss the two subjects most distasteful to her—Lord Howard and Shalimar.

Lady Monteith enjoyed a few moments of high melodrama when, with a long and soulful glance, she passed the lobster patties to Clifford. "I had Cook make these for you," she said. At least the rapscallion had the grace to blush! Clifford looked hopefully toward the footman for the champagne that usually accompanied them, but saw only white wine.

"Lovely, Irene," he said. "Nora makes them a little spicier, but yours are always good."

"It's news to me if anything spicy is to be found at the Willows," she snipped. "I must have been underestimating the cuisine of the Bright ladies. Howard appears to have found something to his taste there as well." After this sledgehammer piece of irony she turned slowly away. No speed was necessary to avoid retaliation; Clifford was a slow top.

At last the leisurely meal was over. Monteith, determined to have the next dance with Samantha, rushed to draw her chair before Mr. Tucker could beat him to it.

"Is your card filled for the next set, Sam?" he asked with seeming casualness.

"You didn't supply cards, Monty."

"But may I have the pleasure?"

"Mama spoke of leaving right after dinner," she said doubtfully, and looked toward her mother and Clifford.

When she saw her mother nodding and handing Clifford

over to Irene for the set, she smiled in relief. "It seems we're going to stay a little longer," she said, and put her trembling fingers on his arm. Monteith placed his fingers over hers and gazed at her with an enigmatic look. "You never arranged the waltzing lessons you promised," she said, to fill the piercing silence.

"I've been remiss, haven't I, Sam?" His brooding eyes spoke of more than waltzing lessons.

Samantha gulped and heard her voice come out in a bleat. "I'm sure you've been busy. You can't think of everything."

"It wasn't for lack of thinking. Merely I was too slow off the mark." A man's voice didn't hum with meaning over such a picayune thing as Monteith was ostensibly discussing.

The sets were forming and they went to join one of the younger groups. Before they had taken two steps, a gruff "Halloa" was heard from the hall beyond. The next sound Samantha heard was a growling profanity from her partner. She looked to the door and saw Howard's dark eyes scanning the room for her. Her instinct was to take her heels and run, but Howard spotted her, and she felt nailed to the floor. She couldn't move. She swallowed convulsively and looked a mute plea to her partner, who was frowning at her peculiar reaction.

"How did he get back so soon?" she asked, but in a purely rhetorical spirit.

Before more could be said, Howard was plunging toward her through the crowd, upsetting all the squares. His rough voice rode loud over the music. "Beating my time, eh, Nevvie? I don't object to your keeping Sam's feet hot for me, as long as you haven't het up anything else. Heh, heh." As he spoke, he put a possessive arm around Samantha's waist.

For an awkward moment she stood pinned between the two gentlemen, each with an arm around her, while the other dancers looked their impatience.

"You'll have to wait your turn, Uncle," Monteith said stiffly.

"I claim the fiancé's privilege!" Howard replied, with a truculent glare.

This was extraordinarily gauche behavior, even from Howard. Samantha suspected he had been drinking rather heavily and foresaw a regular brawl breaking out.

"Another time, Monty," she said, and with an imploring look, she removed his hand from her waist.

With nostrils quivering and eyes narrowed to slits, Monteith replied, "As you wish." He made a curt bow and withdrew.

Howard shook his head. "That lad's like an egg. So full of himself there's no room for anything else. I hope he hasn't been pestering you during my absence."

"The dance, Howard!" she reminded him, and with stumbling steps, Howard began to dance.

"You're back earlier than you expected," she mentioned.

"I couldn't stay away from you, my dear." He smiled. It was a loose-lipped leer. The fumes of whiskey were quite noticeable at this close range. "I finished up my business in a trice and came jauntering back. There wasn't a woman in all of London to touch my gel."

"You were looking, were you?" she asked stiffly.

"Nay, a man with a plate of fresh spring lamb don't go sniffing for mutton. I was true as the North Star."

He, she noticed, was the North Star; she a plate of lamb. Her revulsion grew. If he had been sober, she would have told him on the spot that she didn't intend to marry him. She feared what excesses of bad behavior his insobriety might precipitate. The steps of the dance took them apart and Samantha drew a breath of relief. She noticed Howard staring at her and felt a quiver of apprehension. What outré thing would he say, or do, next?

When they came together again, he said, "I don't see you wearing your engagement ring, my dear."

154

"There is a reason, Howard. We'll discuss it later."

"I always seize the moment." He laughed, and danced her out of the set.

Once free of impediments, he grabbed her hand and hauled her out of the door. Monteith, watching them from the side of the room, came to attention. Howard looked up and down the hallway that was cluttered with strolling couples and headed for a private parlor.

"Where are you going? I want to dance, Howard!" Samantha exclaimed. He paid no heed but hurried her forward. She disliked to create a commotion at Monteith's party, and was forced to go along with him.

Monteith's study was the closest vacant room, and it was there that Howard led her. He snatched up a candelabrum and opened the door.

"I don't want to—"

The door closed behind her with a bang. "Howard, open that door at once!" she demanded.

"I *do* like a gel with spirit." He chuckled and set down the candelabrum, the better to attack her.

As his head lurched above hers, she smelled the stale breath of a long drinking bout. His eyes were bloodshot, and at close range the stubble of incipient whiskers was noticeable. "You're drunk!" she exclaimed, and tried to free herself.

"Drunk with love for you, my pretty," he said softly, and clamped her head with one hand as before, to hold it steady. With the other hand, he pressed her against him.

She watched in horror as his bloodshot eyes and grizzled head swooped down. The prickle of whiskers was immediately followed by the taste of his lustful, whiskey-soaked lips. She shoved at his chest with all her might. Despite his condition, Howard was plenty strong enough to hold her. The dread of interrupting Monteith's party was forgotten. Samantha wrenched her head aside, opened her lips, and hollered, "Help!"

Almost before the word left her mouth, the door was

flung open and Monteith lunged into the room. His face was white with fury as he glanced at the wrestling couple before him. "Get your paws off her!" he growled, hurrying forward.

"Damme, she's my woman. I'll do as I please with her."

Monteith's eyes glittered dangerously, and his hand flashed to Lord Howard's shoulder to fling him back. Samantha watched in horror as Howard gave a sly, challenging grin.

"Fisticuffs, eh, Nevvie?" he said, and clenched his hands to fists, then began dancing in circles around Monteith.

"Don't be ridiculous!" Monteith snarled. "I don't fight old men!"

The hated slur incited Howard to such a fit of passion that he let fly with his right. Monteith was caught on the chin and sent reeling back against a chair.

"Well, I'll be damned!" he said, and blinked in shock. In a flash, he lifted his fists and landed his uncle a facer. Lord Howard went falling backwards, hitting his head on the corner of Monteith's desk as he fell. A hollow crack echoed in the room.

Sam clutched her mouth. "My God, you've killed him," she gasped.

Monteith rounded on her. "I hope you're satisfied!" He paced forward to examine his uncle.

Sam hurried to his side and they both leaned over the prostrate form that lay sprawled on the floor. Lord Howard wore a loose-lipped smile of stupefaction. He was still breathing, but he had never looked unlovelier. And this was the monster she was engaged to marry!

"What happened?" Monteith demanded, after he had examined his uncle and decided he was more drunk than wounded.

"He attacked me."

"What did you expect from your passionate lover? Hand

holding? Sweet nothings in your ear? This was only an appetizer to what will come after the wedding.''

''I shan't marry him! I never intended to!''

Monteith stared as though listening to a lunatic. ''Then you shouldn't have accepted his ring!''

''I didn't! He sent it to the house—I didn't receive it till he was halfway to London. I never said I'd marry him.''

''By God, you never said you wouldn't!''

They both turned to the door at the sound of running footsteps in the hallway. ''Better close the door,'' Monteith said, and hopped up.

As it was Mrs. Bright in the lead, they let her in. Hot on her heels came Lady Monteith and Clifford Sutton.

''What happened?'' Mrs. Bright demanded. ''I saw Lord Howard dragging you off, Sam.''

''I heard the scream,'' Lady Monteith added. She espied Lord Howard on the floor and flew forward to tend him. ''Close the door, Clifford,'' she called over her shoulder. Clifford, long accustomed to do her bidding, closed the door.

''Is he drunk?'' Lady Monteith asked.

Monteith said, ''Yes,'' at the same moment as Sam said ''No.''

Monteith gave her a quelling stare, which his mother noticed. ''Drunk, is it? And what, may I ask, accounts for the bruise on his chin? What really happened?''

''He attacked Sam,'' Monty told her, with an apologetic glance at her mother.

''The man's a monster!'' Mrs. Bright said, and went to console her daughter.

Lady Monteith shook her head and gave a brisk *tsk*. ''He is a rake. I thought my husband was bad. Well, he *was*, Monty, but not even Ernest ever attacked an innocent girl. Not to say that you are blameless, Samantha, leading him on. What did you expect, my girl, that he'd wrap you up in cotton wool? He's no Clifford Sutton, to be satisfied

157

with a hug and a squeeze," she added, with a satirical squint at her former beau.

"We'd best get him to bed," Monteith said.

"I'll not have his carcass hauled through the house with the whole neighborhood gawking," his mother decreed. "We'll bundle him in blankets and leave him here."

"I'll tie and gag him, in case he comes to," her son added, pulling out his handkerchief to begin the job.

"Too farouche, Monty," his mother objected. "Put the brandy decanter on the floor beside him. If he comes to, he'll drink himself into a stupor."

Clifford looked on in disapproving amazement. "Perhaps we should call a doctor. . . ." he suggested.

Lady Monteith took a closer look at the body on the floor. She tapped Howard's cheeks, then lifted his eyelids to peer in at his eyes. "Not necessary," she announced. "Some blankets and a pillow, Clifford. Get the throw from my little parlor, and the embroidered pillows—the old ones I use to brace my back. I don't want him casting up his accounts on the new ones."

Again, Clifford went off to do as he was told. Within minutes, Lord Howard was the most comfortable one in the room. He was beginning to murmur in a way that indicated no serious damage.

Lady Monteith rubbed her hands. "That's that, then. Shall we return to the dance?"

"Samantha will want to go home," Clifford said. "We'll take her."

Monteith looked at Samantha. Samantha looked at Howard. Mrs. Bright looked at Monteith looking at her daughter. "Perhaps it will look more natural if we remain awhile, Clifford. You were having your dance with Irene. Why don't you go on with it? I was just going to the refreshment parlor for a glass of wine."

They went about their interrupted pleasures. Monteith and Samantha were the last to go. He blew out the candles and turned the key in the lock as he left. He looked a question at Samantha. "I don't imagine you want to return to the dance," he said.

"I think not."

"You're looking a little pale. Can I get you—" But Mrs. Bright was in the refreshment parlor. "A breath of air, perhaps?"

"That would be nice," she said, and smiled her gratitude.

They went out through the library to avoid the crowds, into the moonlit rose garden. They strolled toward the rippling fountain, with a foot of space between them, not speaking. Now that they were alone, a dreadful constraint had fallen over them. At the first bench, they stopped, as if by prearrangement. The scent of roses perfumed the air. The ghastly paleness of each blossom was limned against black leaves in the shadowy night.

"I expect it's for me to apologize for my uncle," Monteith said stiffly.

"It wasn't your fault. Monty, what should I do? Would it be cowardly to turn him off with a note?"

"There's no need for you to have any further connection with him. Let your mother write the note. Howard was raised a gentleman, whatever he has become since. He'll know the romance is terminated."

"I have to return his ring."

"I'll do it."

"I can't go on avoiding him forever. He plans to settle in the neighborhood. I want it finished with the least ill will possible."

"Some hostility is bound to linger after tonight's proceedings. With luck, Howard might have forgotten the details by morning."

"Oh, dear, then he'll think we're still engaged!"

His jaw stiffened and one eyebrow rose. "Did I misunderstand you earlier? You said you hadn't accepted him."

"I didn't accept! I just didn't refuse—exactly."

159

"No wonder the poor man was confused. I really can't understand your actions in this matter, Sam. You led me to believe you had accepted him when I—when I spoke to you at the Willows."

"When you forbade the match, you mean!" Her voice became hot at the memory of that ill-fated visit.

"Now you see the wisdom of my trying to discourage you."

"I never dreamed he would be this bad! Oh, I wish he had never come home!" she said, and blinked a tear from the corner of her eye.

Monteith stood a moment, thinking. Then he drew out a handkerchief. "Come now, it's not that bad," he said. "Howard was only alone with you a moment." He gently dabbed at the tear and smiled. "One can hardly blame him, you know, for wanting to kiss you." He lifted her chin till she was gazing at him. The moonlight caressed her troubled young face and reflected from the depths of her dark eyes. An encouraging smile trembled on her lips. "I'd like to myself, if I could be sure you wouldn't holler for help. Folks say the only thing to do after being thrown from a horse is to remount at once, or you'll have a life-long fear of riding. I expect the same applies to being mauled by an Indian."

Her nervous quiver encouraged Monteith to try his luck. Fearful of frightening her, he pulled her into his arms gently, waiting to see if she objected. When she voluntarily lifted her arms and placed them on his shoulders, he crushed her against him and sought her lips. The careful gentleness swiftly escalated to passion, as all memory of Lord Howard's awful attack was washed clean by Monteith's scalding embrace. She felt a pulsating weakness invade her body, yet discovered strength to return the pressure of his lips. Her hands found the proud column of his neck, reveled in the masculine texture of sinew and bone and flesh. For a long moment they clung together; then Monteith lifted his head and gazed at her.

An incipient smile lit his eyes. "That wasn't so bad, was it?"

"Help!" she whispered, and buried her face comfortably in the crook of his shoulder, waiting to hear a declaration of his intentions.

A soft ripple of laughter echoed above her. "Don't worry; help is on the way. We'll all need a hand if Howard remembers anything of tonight."

Sam looked at him, surprised and disappointed that his thoughts had returned to Howard at this juncture. "He can't hold it against you that I jilted him."

"You haven't formally jilted him yet—but I have knocked him unconscious. I rather think Howard will include me in his ill humor. Unless . . ."

"You're still currying to the nabob!" she exclaimed.

He smiled a soft smile. "Be a little patient, Sam. We haven't heard the epilogue yet. Why employ a blunt instrument when a scalpel might sever the bond more cleanly, and with much less loss of blood? I'll drop by the Willows tomorrow to pick up Howard's ring."

Samantha tossed her head angrily. "Very well."

"There is still Mama to be conciliated. She's in the boughs over losing Clifford. You can see what a deal of ill will would be let loose if we should complicate matters by doing something rash. As you pointed out, we want to do the thing with the minimum of fuss and bother."

Sam examined his enigmatic face and found she had very little idea what he was talking about. What was quite clear was that he had no intention of offering for her. The auspicious moment had come and gone. The upshot of it all seemed to be that she was to break with Howard, but not to gain a replacement fiancé. Monteith had managed to get exactly what he wanted.

She rose briskly and straightened her skirt. "I shall expect you in the morning to pick up Howard's ring," she said.

"You may be very sure I shan't forget that happy errand."

With a look of triumph, he put his hand on her elbow and led her back inside. Sam remembered she had the ring in her reticule, but said nothing about it.

Chapter 16

In the morning parlor at the Willows, sunlight gleamed on the silver coffeepot and glinted in snow-white china. Beyond the window and through the leaves of the mulberry tree, the top of High Street was visible and already busy. The ladies had slept in late after the fête champêtre. The party was considered a great success by most of Lambrook. Mrs. Bright smiled to see Mr. Beazely approach the Armstrong house bearing a bouquet of posies.

She drew a contented sigh and set down her coffee cup. "Good things come in threes," she said. "Here are you rid of Lord Howard and expecting an offer from Monteith."

"I am not expecting an offer, Mama!"

"I made sure when you went into the garden with Monteith last night . . ."

"I didn't go to receive an offer. Nothing of the sort happened."

In her happiness, Mrs. Bright found a reason for the delay. "He could hardly offer till you rid yourself of Howard. I shall get busy and write up that note right after breakfast. That is the first good thing. Secondly, I shouldn't be at all surprised if Clifford offers for me after you are shot off. And thirdly, Mr. Beazely wouldn't be calling at ten o'clock in the morning if he were not becoming serious about Mrs. Armstrong. Mark my words, Sam, she'll nab him. At last we shall know what class of society she belongs in. He will be an excellent match, so well to grass and very respectable. No doubt she is feeling emanations this very minute. He'll bring the fortune-telling to a halt.''

Samantha let her mother babble on, as it saved her having to talk herself. She was in no mood for polite chitchat.

At Lambrook Hall, Lady Monteith presided over a much grander table in a much grander room. None of the grandeur gave her any pleasure that day. Her thoughts were gloomy as she sat at breakfast with her son. In fact, she was hardly thinking at all, but only trying unsuccessfully to contain her seething emotions.

"I hope you are not hinting that you mean to marry Samantha Bright yourself!" she declared, eyes flashing. "Have some pride, Monteith. To go hat in hand to those wretched women, after what they have done to us!"

In a good mood, Monteith replied mildly. "The damage has been largely undone, Mama. Sam is giving Howard his congé. This little illness will slow down his search for a replacement. With luck, the building of Shalimar will consume his energy for the next months. You said last night you wished to repair the rent friendship with Nora—"

"That was last night. And furthermore, your uncle doesn't remember a thing about that disgraceful interlude in your study. He speaks quite as foolishly as ever about Samantha. Don't think to announce an engagement between Sam and yourself, when the whole town thinks she is engaged to Howard—including Howard. I'm surprised he isn't on his way to the Willows already, ill though he is. Really, he looks a total wreck today. One trembles to think what dissipations he has been indulging in in London. He tells me lemon water will cure him, but I am sending off for Dr. Pratt if he shows no improvement by noon.''

Monteith drew out his watch and glanced at it impatiently. "I had planned to leave immediately and speak to Mrs. Bright. She will be sending Howard a letter terminating that foolish misalliance, and Sam will be returning the ring."

"Not when the poor man is ill, Monteith. You must show a little consideration. Only think if his dyspepsia were to carry him off," she said half hopefully. "I wonder if he has made a will. One dislikes to ask . . ."

Through the rose tints of his euphoria, Monteith recognized that it would be cruel to kick a fellow when he was down. "Let's send for the doctor immediately," he suggested.

A footman was sent off, and within half an hour Dr. Pratt was being led up the stairs with his gold-knobbed cane in one hand and his black bag in the other. It was another thirty minutes before he returned belowstairs. Such a lengthy visit gave rise to awful hopes and fears. Lady Monteith had soared in fancy from the dizzying heights of being sole inheritor of the nabob's wealth to being left out in the cold entirely. She was frazzled to a thread by the time the visit was over.

Dr. Pratt wore a serious face when he went to join her and Monteith for consultation. "I don't like the looks of this," he said, shaking his head. "His temperature is over a hundred, and his pulse very weak and rapid."

"Surely a little too much brandy couldn't have caused that!" Lady Monteith said.

Monteith felt a dreadful premonition that a crack on the head might be the cause, but was soon reassured.

"No, a lot too much, over a long period of time. Liver, complicated with a fever, I've come across before in gentlemen returned from India. Something they pick up there," he said, rubbing his jaw in confusion. "It flares up from time to time."

Lady Monteith leaned forward in her chair and spoke in a hollow voice. "Is it likely to prove fatal?" she asked.

"It shortens the life, but it don't seem to carry them off

165

in one blow. It recurs, getting worse over the years. Cutting down on the brandy and wine would help stave it off. His constitution should be built up—plenty of rest, no late nights. I fancy his late-night revels do half the mischief. And don't let him eat those spiced dishes the nabobs like so well.''

"Try if you can stop him!'' Monteith said.

"I put the fear of God into him,'' Dr. Pratt replied. "He'll eat pap and gruel and pork jelly for the next week, and like it. His liver is giving him such a hard time, I shouldn't think he'll cut up too stiff on you. He has a great desire to live, you see. That is better than a tonic. I daresay it is his engagement that causes it. At least, he speaks a deal about Miss Bright.''

Lady Monteith bared her teeth in a parody of a smile. Life was too cruel. The one good thing that had come out of the fête champêtre, the rupture of Howard's engagement, was back to haunt her. On the other hand, it kept Monteith from offering for Sam. How odd that she used to wish the girl was her daughter-in-law.

"I've written up some instructions,'' Dr. Pratt said, drawing out a sheet of paper. "But the most important things are plenty of rest and quiet, and no brandy or wine. Mild foods only. I'll be back tomorrow to see how the old gentleman goes on. You'll call me if he takes a turn for the worse. And now I'm off to change George Plummer's bandage. He nearly cut his foot off with an axe, clumsy fellow.''

When the doctor was gone, Monteith sat staring into space, planning how to arrange his immediate future. Naturally, he couldn't propose to Sam immediately, but he could drop a hint.

"Well, that settles it,'' his mother said. "You must explain the situation to the Brights. Nora will not expect you to offer for Sam now.''

"It's not Nora I'm worried about.''

"You might worry about your mother, for once. Financial interests aside, think how you would look, beating up an old man—your own uncle—then stealing his bride while he is sick in his bed, possibly dying."

"Neither the 'beating,' which was exactly one blow, nor the fever are my fault."

"Next you will say offering for Sam is not your fault, either. Hah, I know whose fault it is. The sly minx. You were properly taken in. She never had any intention of marrying that old gaffer. She only accepted to nudge you into offering."

"She never accepted at all."

"But she took the ring fast enough!"

"There's no point arguing, Mama. I'll go to the Brights' now and explain the situation here."

"Give my regards to Mr. Sutton," his mother said tartly.

After Monteith left, she took a pot of tea and a novel upstairs and read to Howard for an hour. He found it strangely peaceful, lying in bed, looking out at the pale blue sky of England, dappled with the tips of tall trees. So different from India. There it was blazing blue and scorching sun or the demmed monsoons, when the air was as heavy and gray as the sky.

"It's peaceful to be home, Irene." He smiled wanly. "Many a sultry night as I lay on my *charpoy,* I dreamed of such peace. But when I got home, there was so much I wanted to crowd into what is left of my life that I went into a sort of frenzy. Dashing off here and there—to London. I fear I overdid it this visit. Next time I shall stay away from the Green Room."

"So that's what you were up to, naughty boy," she scolded, but leniently. Of course an older woman understood a man's needs. Especially Irene—she had learned about men the hard way, from his brother Ernest.

"You have danced your jig, sir; now you must pay the piper. But we shall try to make your recuperation as pleasant as possible."

"I'd like to see Sam. I fear she isn't happy with the ring I gave her. I daresay it was the star ruby she had in her eye. I only gave her the smaller ruby set with diamonds."

"What were you keeping the star ruby for?"

"I thought it a trifle gaudy for a young girl. I planned to give it to you in thanks for your hospitality."

A beatific smile curved Irene's lips. She held the teacup for Howard to sip. Her voice was a dovelike coo of pleasure. "You are thoughtful! I never expected anything of the sort."

"I always had the greatest respect and admiration for Ernest's bride. If your memory is as long as mine, you will recall who was dangling after her first."

Irene did, indeed, recall. She recalled as well the abrupt manner of tuning him off once Ernest began showing his interest. "My parents were at me night and day, Howard. You know how ambitious they always were."

"I understand, Irene. I daresay I'd have done the same thing in your boots. I was a callow, penniless youth at the time, with my fortune to be made, and Ernie was already in command of the hill. And now we're old, you and I. A young bride will give me the illusion of youth for the few years I have left. She is monstrous pretty, young Sammie."

"Lovely." Lady Monteith smiled through her rage. "I only hope she doesn't wear you out."

When the visit was over, she went to her room and attacked her face with the rouge pot. Or was it the hair that made him think her old? Silver wings were forming around the temples. She would have her dresser buy a bottle of henna dye. And perhaps a rearrangement of her coiffure . . .

Samantha could see at a glance that Monteith was troubled when he came to call. "How is Howard?" she asked, when he was seated in the saloon.

"He's taken a turn for the worse," he said, and outlined the situation. "Mama feels—and I'm afraid I agree with her—that this isn't the optimum time for you to turn him off."

"Surely you're not suggesting I go on being engaged to him!" she exclaimed in horror.

"You needn't worry about any recrudescence of his passion. He's flat on his back—weak as a newborn kitten. It will be just for a few days. As soon as he's feeling stouter, you can jilt him."

Sam looked at her mother. Mrs. Bright pinched her lips and considered for a moment. "Monteith is right, Sam. You can't tell him when the doctor says the engagement is all that is keeping up his spirits. You must be patient for a few days."

A second thinking of the matter led Sam to agree. "You're right, of course. What difference does a few days make after all? And as he is ill, I shan't have to call on him."

"Not today, in any case," Monteith decided.

By the next day, Howard felt well enough to sit up and eat a bowl of gruel for breakfast. It was fed to him by a much-rejuvenated Lady Monteith. Her hair, arranged in a youthful bundle of curls atop her head, gleamed like new copper. Her cheeks were as pink as peonies, and on her finger sat a heavy star ruby, given in a fit of gratitude the night before when she had read him three boring chapters of Scott's *Waverley*.

"More *Waverley*, Howard?" she asked archly when the tray had been removed.

"Let us just sit and talk, if you can spare me a few minutes, my dear."

"You know my time is entirely at your disposal."

Howard took her fingers and squeezed them. "I have been a great thundering nuisance to you, Irene. And now

169

this to top it off—an invalid on your hands. You will be wishing me at Jericho.''

"Where else should you come after your travels, but to your home, Howard? I'll hear no more of nuisances, if you please. What have I to do all day long, alone as I am nine-tenths of the time? I am delighted with your company.''

"Do the youngsters not visit you? I had hoped to see Ted and Bert before now.''

"Had they known you were coming, Howard, wild horses wouldn't have kept them away. They are touring the Lake District this summer. Monteith thinks they should see their own country, to develop a proper feeling for it and all its beauty. We've written, and hope to see them soon.''

"Ah, well, I hope they don't come till I am feeling more the thing. Youngsters racketing around a house are the very devil, but I do want to speak to them later on and see what I can do for them. I thought twenty-five thousand apiece would see them settled in whatever careers they have in mind.''

A gush of pure joy made Irene's rouge unnecessary. "Oh, Howard, you are too generous! Fifty thousand pounds!'' In her excitement, she reached forward and grabbed his hands. He squeezed hers and took advantage of her proximity to slip a kiss on her cheek. Soft as a baby's skin, that cheek. And what a pretty flowery smell came from her.

"The least I can do for my nevvies.''

And the least Irene could do was keep them out of his way while he was ill. There was no point risking the fortune by having the ill-bred whelps where Howard could see them. It hadn't taken Monteith long to come to cuffs with the nabob, and he was the most civilized of her sons.

Receiving gifts and money always put Lady Monteith in high spirits. She could hardly control her joy that morning. She became quite frolicsome just before dashing downstairs to write the notes telling her younger sons to prolong their tour.

"Let me straighten these pillows," she said, lifting Howard's head in her two soft hands.

He grabbed her fingers. "Why are you so kind to an old sinner like me, Irene?" he asked. His dark eyes gleamed with the stirring of passion.

She suppressed her joy and allowed a wistful smile to do its work. "We shan't have you with us much longer, Howard. Soon your marble walls will be rising."

"I shall miss Lambrook Hall. Remember, we used to chase the peacocks, Irene? I pulled a feather from old Inky's tail and gave it to you. Papa gave me a sound thrashing. You no longer have peacocks in the park."

"I remember," she said, on a luxurious sigh. "No, the peacocks are gone."

"I shall give you a pair—and come and visit them often, if I may."

"I wish you never had to leave."

Irene was careful not to look at Howard as she uttered this lure. She busied herself straightening his blankets, and as she left the room the feminine swaying of hips was a little more pronounced than usual.

Howard watched her departure with admiring eyes. A fine figure of a woman, always was. In his weakened condition, the upheaval of building Shalimar seemed like a hideously bothersome and expensive business. How nice it would be to finish his days here at the Hall, or someplace like it.

As to a young bride and a parcel of sons—children were noisy, troublesome wretches. His little lad in India—Georgie, he called him—had squalled night and day from the minute he was born. His lineage lived on in Ernest's sons. It was not as though he had a title of his own to bequeath.

Of course, Irene was a widow. As that handsome hussy, Serena, said, a woman was not a suit of clothes ordered for one man, but a book to be read. For that matter, he had often worn Ernie's jackets and been quite comfortable in them. Sammie was as pretty as could stare, but a prudish young lady. The young didn't understand passion. It would take months to heat up her ardor. He could hardly jilt her—Mrs. Bright was Irene's best friend. Monteith seemed rather fond of the young lady. . . .

His eyes fluttered shut and he wafted in dreams back to Kashmir, where he wandered through the gardens of Shalimar with Jemdanee.

Monteith noticed his mother's juvenescence and had some notion of its cause. It was the fifty thousand for the boys and the great ruby ring that she spoke of, but her smiles looked like million-pound smiles. The solution to every problem lay in his mother's being able to pull it off. He personally went to the bookstall and picked up half a dozen romantic novels and a pot of rouge of a less glaring red.

Chapter 17

Two days after the fête, Monteith went to the Willows to deliver Sam to the Hall for her first visit to the invalid.

"Don't leave me alone with him, Monteith!" Sam warned, as she put on her bonnet at the hall mirror.

"You'll find him a changed man," Monteith promised. "I'm almost beginning to like him myself." He tilted her bonnet at a more fashionable angle and gazed at her with a long, unsettling look. "Don't worry I'll leave you alone. You might find yourself falling under his spell again."

"That would upset your plans, wouldn't it?" She sniffed.

"More than you know."

"I never was under his spell."

"I swear Mama is. Of course, his kind donation to the boys has something to do with it."

They went to the carriage and in due course entered the grounds of Lambrook Hall. Samantha looked at the stretching sea of lawns and the spreading breeches, with the stone walls of the Hall rising in the distance. "How lovely it is here." She sighed.

"I mean to spend more time at home in the future."

"A city rattle like you? Dr. Johnson says when a man is tired of London, he's tired of life."

"Dr. Johnson is wrong. I am not tired of life; I'm only tired of wasting it. This illness of Howard's has made me realize I'm mortal."

"That must have come as a sore blow," she said curtly.

"Most knowledge is hard gained. Being only mortal and with a mortal's wish for eternity, I mean to marry and populate the county with my offspring."

"In that order, I hope?"

"In that order, if Howard is well enough to receive your rejection," he said, and cast a meaningful smile at his partner. "Otherwise . . . well, I don't mean to wait much longer."

Sam stared at him, a hopeful question burning in her eyes.

"I *did* mention the epilogue, didn't I?"

"I wish you wouldn't speak in riddles," Sam said coldly, and turned her attention to the swallows screeching above as they darted from tree to tree.

Samantha hardly recognized Lady Monteith when she met her in the saloon. What had wrought this change? Her eyes and cheeks glowed, but not so noticeably as her henna hair. Her toilette, too, was livelier than before. She hadn't quite sunk to sprigged muslin at her years, but she wore a pretty gown of emerald green that reminded Sam of the lawns just admired, and Howard of Kashmir.

"How kind of you to come," Lady Monteith said. Sam's uncertain position had robbed her of vitality. Lady Monteith's heart soared to see such slender competition. Even a distressed young maiden was still plenty attractive, however, and further measures were called for.

"Try to cheer him up," she said. "Make him laugh, if you can. You go with her, Monty. Howard will like to hear the lively chatter of you youngsters. Urge him to talk about building Shalimar and filling it with children."

Howard had admitted his dread of this project. Peace and quiet were what he spoke of now. "Stay as long as you can. He has trouble getting in the days," she added, as a final deterrent.

Though the ordeal loomed with all the attraction of a visit to the tooth drawer for Sam, she gamely attempted to carry out instructions, as she felt guilty about breaking the engagement. Monteith knew his mother well enough to recognize her scheme. He thoroughly approved of her intentions and was ready to abet her. He opened the door and entered the sickroom with a loud "Holloa, Uncle. See who I've brought to entertain you."

Lord Howard sank deeper into his pillows and assumed a sickly air without too much trouble. His pallor was not the sickly white of a normal invalid, but a bright yellow, due to his liverish condition and the results of long exposure to the tropical sun. "Sammie, kind of you to come," he said in a puling whine.

"Good morning, Howard. I trust you are feeling better." She smiled.

"Not as fit as I would like."

"Why, you'll be up and about in no time," Monteith said heartily, and sat on the edge of his uncle's bed with a lurch that sent the mattess bobbing. "You must be back on your pegs for next week's assembly. Sam is looking forward to having a jig with you."

Samantha looked at the wreck before her and felt grave misgivings as to Monteith's attitude. But she really felt sorry for Howard and wanted to cheer him.

"I'll save you every dance," she promised rashly. Monteith is going to set up waltzing lessons, if you please."

"I have seen the waltz done in London. I'm not sure I approve of it for ladies."

"Gentlemen can hardly perform it alone!" Sam said, and laughed.

"They can perform it with the other sort of woman," Howard pointed out. Sam's face took on an expression of shocked disapproval. Irene would have laughed and teased him. The young were really tediously self-righteous. He had convinced himself he must be rid of Miss Bright and decided to show her the rough side of his nature. "Gentlemen are allowed some latitude in such matters," he said haughtily.

Sam looked warily to Monteith, to see if he concurred with this notion. He nodded his agreement, but when she caught his eyes, she noted the glint of mischief. "I must disagree, Howard!" she said firmly. "*My* husband will not carry on with lightskirts, I promise you."

"Children, children," Monteith said. "It's time for a glass of wine to clear the air."

He went to the door and let out a bellow that sent Howard into a grimace. "None for me. The doctor has got me on infants' fare," Howard said.

"A glass of wine won't do you any harm," his nephew said.

"Much you know about it! It could kill me. You wouldn't believe how my poor gut gripes at anything sour." He rubbed his stomach and frowned in imaginary pain as he spoke. He'd make sure the bottle stayed behind when the youngsters left.

Monteith chattered inanely and loudly as he filled two glasses. "A toast to the handsome couple," he said, clinking Sam's glass and smiling at Howard.

He then turned his attention to relating some long and not very amusing stories, which sent both himself and Sam off into peals of noisy laughter. Sam noticed that the louder they laughed and talked, the less happy Howard became.

"I fear we're tiring you, Howard," she said after half an hour that had seemed much longer.

"I could do with some quiet," he said weakly. "Thank you for coming, Sam. You mustn't put yourself out too much on my account. Visits are tiring. You youngsters have better things to do than sit with a sick old man."

"You're not old!" she told him. But he seemed to

have aged twenty years since his first coming to the Hall.

"I fear I am, my dear. That promise I so rashly made you at Shalimar—I may have to renege on it. You recall what I said, about my gray hair. . . ."

She gave a blush and lowered her eyes. Prude, Howard thought. "You run along, Nevvie," he said to Monteith. Samantha bit her lower lip and looked alert.

Monteith looked a question to her. She nodded, and he left.

"Draw your chair closer to my bed," Howard suggested.

She nudged the chair an inch closer, ready to flee at the first sign of passion. "What is it, Howard?" she asked stiffly.

"Nay, there's no need to freeze on me, lass. It's time you and I admitted the truth. We don't suit. I'm too old, and you're too young. It will be a disappointment to you now, but in time you'll get over it. I'll see what I can do to hint Monteith in your direction. If you can lose that missish way of pokering up at any mention of sex, you might nab him. He ain't a nabob, but he's got a handle to his name, and the Hall is a fine little house."

A wave of relief inundated Samantha. She felt as if she had been released from prison. "If you're sure, Howard . . ."

"It's a pity, but facts are facts. Winter and summer don't belong together. I waited too long to come home. I shan't be building Shalimar after all. I daresay that was half what attracted you to me."

"No, to tell the truth, I wasn't attracted by Shalimar at all. I thought it sounded silly." She drew the heavy ring from her finger and handed it to him.

He shoved it back, saying, "Keep it as a reminder of me."

"As if I needed a reminder!" she exclaimed.

Howard felt a proud swelling of his chest and smiled

177

benignly. "Call it a little something for the trouble and disappointment I've caused you."

"I couldn't keep it. It's too valuable," she said firmly, and set it on the table.

"As you wish, my dear. So it is good-bye," he said, with a sad smile, and an eye to the table to see the level of the wine bottle.

"Yes, it is good-bye, dear Howard."

Assured of her freedom, she risked a very quick kiss on his forehead. It felt hot and dry, and nearly as repulsive as his lips. Then she rose and glided quietly from the room.

Monteith was waiting for her in the hallway. "Well?" he asked.

"Monty, he jilted me!" she whispered, and fell into a fit of nervous giggles.

He lifted her in his arms and swung her around in the air, with her feet ten inches off the ground. "Then we can make it official. You're my woman!" he said.

He gazed into her face, hovering above his, then lowered her till their lips met in a frenzied kiss. His lips moved restively as her arms tightened around his neck. The long kiss continued as she slid slowly to the floor, gliding against him in a body caress.

When at last he released her, she looked shyly at him. "Is that what you've been waiting for all this time?" she asked. "For Howard to jilt me?"

"We foolish gentlemen have a code in these matters. Stealing another man's bride is frowned upon. I've wanted to make my declaration for days. I was within a breath of it that afternoon in your saloon, but somehow we came to cuffs instead. I was jealous as a green cow."

"And I was mad as a hornet. I thought it was only my getting Howard's fortune that upset you."

"No, it was Howard's getting you. But enough of that, I want to rush in and make it official, before someone else gets at you. I love you madly, darling. Will you do me the honor—oh, damme, I haven't asked your mother for permission."

"She says yes," Sam assured him.

The happy couple were embracing in a way that Lady Monteith found highly improper when she spotted them on her way upstairs to listen at Howard's door.

"Monteith!" she exclaimed loudly.

"We've done it, Mama. He broke the engagement."

Lady Monteith's eyes darted to Sam's ringless finger, and a small smile formed. "I'll just look in and see if he requires anything," she said.

She found Howard with the wine bottle to his lips, smiling like a pagan. "Come sit beside me and console me, Irene," he tempted, patting the bed.

She spotted the diamond-and-ruby ring sitting on the side table as she perched on the mattress. "The doctor said no wine, Howard dear," she reminded him.

"Just a drop to wet my whistle. I am feeling much stronger since you have been taking such good care of me."

"What are sisters for?" she asked archly.

One of Howard's hands slid toward the ring on the table, the other around Irene's waist. "I never thought of you as a sister, Irene. Lately I have come to think of you as a very desirable woman." He reached for her left hand, from which her wedding ring had magically vanished two days ago, for Howard hadn't said anything about overcoming his dread of widows and it seemed ill-advised to remind him of her status.

"You're not forgetting I was married to Ernest?" she asked.

Despite her second-hand condition she looked as good as new—better. "I wager there are pages Ernie hasn't read," he said. Such was his notion of romance that he told her Serena's theory of widows; such was Irene's that she laughed heartily, even though he had told her the circumstances under which Serena had delivered her theory.

Irene wagged her finger and charged him approvingly with being a wee bit of a libertine.

"You bring out the beast in me," he threatened. As the ring was slid onto her finger, the beast drew her into his arms for a tussle that made Irene forget all about Ernest.

After this brief lapse from propriety, Irene returned to business. "We shan't tell the youngsters for a few days," she said. With an unwonted dash of charity, she added, "Miss Bright will be all cut up," to make him feel good.

Howard nodded. "She will. I mean to hint Monteith in that direction to soften the blow. Otherwise we might have to sit a month before she attached someone else. There's no denying the young lady is a prude. I don't know about you, Irene, but my feeling is that the sooner we get on with the wedding, the better."

Irene considered her options and was willing to sacrifice Monteith. There was no saying how long Howard's infatuation would last. He was getting stronger every day. If he recovered enough to jaunter off to London again, he was lost. Best to take him while she had the chance. And, really, she quite liked Sam.

"I'll speak to Monteith. I shouldn't be surprised if he agreed to have her."

"He acted a little jealous the other night at the party, I thought."

"Where shall we live, Howard?" she asked, with an innocent face that gave no hint this decision had been made days ago.

"We'll build ourselves a little hut on the river."

She smiled as though suddenly struck by inspiration. "Howard, you have already purchased the Langford property—why not live there, in that lovely stone mansion? It will be big enough for us two."

"It will do for a start, at least, and we'll buy a grander place in London. You will want to spend the season in London, I daresay. I do like the situation of the Langford cottage, there on the water. We'll have our little fleet of *masulahs* and the temple backing against the orchard.''

"You must teach me to sail."

"There's plenty I mean to teach you, my little hussy." He grinned and pounced on her.

Epilogue

"Age before beauty," Mrs. Bright conceded with a demure smile when the schedule of weddings was being discussed at Lambrook Hall with Lady Monteith. "By all means, you and Howard must go first, Irene. We don't want to risk your losing out on another parti due to dragging your feet. Will you have the wedding here, or will Howard be well enough to hobble to a church?"

Nothing fazed Lady Monteith these days. She smiled gloatingly. "Howard wants to be married at St. Michael's. As to his health, he is well enough to want to go to Paris."

"While Shalimar is being built, you mean?"

"Shalimar be damned. We shall live in the Langford mansion. My pride doesn't require a marble monument, but my common sense does demand a well-run estate. And there will be no fleet of silly foreign boats, either. I shall allow him one good sturdy yacht. The boys will enjoy that when they come to visit."

"Will you allow them to view the naughty Indian temple?"

"If they care to pry open the crates, they may view anything they like. I didn't raise a parcel of prudes. Howard feels a reproduction of a Norman chapel will suit the landscape better and is not planning to erect the temple."

"Howard's taste is improving under your tutelage."

"True." The lady smiled. "But you must not say so in

front of Samantha. And when will you and Clifford tie the knot?"

"Sam and Monteith will go first. Clifford wants Sam to be our matron of honor, and till she is married, you know . . ."

"You mean Mrs. Tucker wants the dignity of having Lady Monteith take part in the ceremony. Dear me, how odd to think of little Sam assuming my title."

"And you being plain Lady Howard."

"Lady Howard will do fine for me. The demotion hasn't stopped the Duke of Rutledge from inviting Ted and Bert to his estate for a couple of weeks. He has more daughters than he knows what to do with, and every one of them has an excellent dot."

This bitter pill was swallowed, and Mrs. Bright proceeded to other touchy matters. "What will you wear for the wedding, Irene? Clifford wants me to wear white. Are you . . ."

A snort of laughter rang out. "White, at our age? We would look a pair of quizzes, and where would we ever wear a white gown again?"

"I have convinced him that pale blue is more becoming to me."

"I've chosen green."

"Do you really think, with that red hair . . ."

"Henna. Monty says he can get me a more natural hue in London."

Mrs. Bright patted her own graying locks and looked uncertainly at her friend.

"It isn't your color, Nora. I should think ash-blond might do. I have the list of colors here somewhere. I'll ring for a servant to get it. Tea, while we're at it, or would you prefer wine?"

The shared problem of setting on a wedding style that would please their husbands without setting the rest of the parish reeling with laughter helped return the old friends to their former good relations. Before the visit was over, plans were afoot for many shared outings.

Monteith and Sam, passing by the open door, exchanged satisfied smiles. "I told you things would sort themselves out." Monty assured her. "Mama is up to anything."

"We shan't have to wait long to make our wedding plans." Sam sighed happily.

"It's been too long to suit me already," Monteith said, and pulled her into his study for a kiss. It was the same room where the nabob had tried to have his way with her. The nature of the attack, too, was quite similar, but it stirred no unpleasant memories. Sam was sufficiently in love to do more than tolerate his amorous assault.

They didn't stop, but did take a short break when the familiar "Holloa" was heard in the hall beyond. "Where's my little woman? Irene? Ranji has arrived. You must come and meet him."

The sound of footfalls was followed by a delighted exclamation from Irene. "Our *dubash*! How lovely! Did he get the quotations for the jewelry collection as you asked?"

The young lovers found the English language more enjoyable. "Shall we go out and join your papa?" Sam suggested.

"Yes, let's," Monteith said, and released her. "We can't abandon Howard. He hasn't a chance against Mama. The poor man needs all the help he can get."

They went arm in arm into the marble-floored entrance hall just as Lady Monteith reached for the quotations and studied them with a contented smile. "This calls for champagne!" she exclaimed. "And a nice cup of tea for you, Howard dear. Holloa, boy!"

Regency presents the popular and prolific...

JOAN SMITH

By the year 2000, 2 out of 3 Americans could be illiterate.

It's true.

Today, 75 million adults...about one American in three, can't read adequately. And by the year 2000, U.S. News & World Report envisions an America with a literacy rate of only 30%.

Before that America comes to be, you can stop it...by joining the fight against illiteracy today.

Call the Coalition for Literacy at toll-free **1-800-228-8813** and volunteer.

**Volunteer
Against Illiteracy.
The only degree you need
is a degree of caring.**

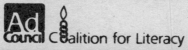

Ad Council   Coalition for Literacy

LV-2